Acknowledge.

I need to give a very special thanks to some very special people. I am so blessed to have a support team that rivals the best teams out there! Thanks a ton to Maria Frisby, my friend, my editor, and my helper extraordinaire!

Thanks to my amazing husband Robert, who has supported me all along the way! Babe, I would be a bit lost without your constant encouragement. Thanks to Tyson deVries for making my beautiful cover art! You are amazing! Also, thanks to my dear friend Amy deVries, for helping along the way and for letting your talented hubby work extra hours to help get this all done. To all of you, thanks for the sacrifice.

Thanks to my kiddos for putting up with the times Mom was mentally lost in her book, and for being so supportive, even when it meant you had to find your own socks.

Thanks so much Diana Phillips for all the kayak trips where we talked about fictional people instead of our real lives! And thanks for letting us use your home for the photo shoot! I love you friend!

Thanks to beautiful Grace Phillips for modeling the cover art! You were perfect!

Thanks so much to my awesome group of first readers. I am so thankful for all of you wonderful people! You all made me better!

Finally, thanks to my amazing God who is the One who put it all together! What would I do without you, Lord? I would be nothing but lost!

One mistake.

One moment of weakness.

Can the love and grace shown by the residents of a small coastal town change the life of a tormented teenager? Can God use this community to convey a model of reconciliation and renewed hope to those the frightened girl had left in her wake?

It Is Well

An Anna James Town Novel

By Amy Johnson

Table of Contents

Chapter 1

Who cared if she looked like an idiot? But, at what point was it okay to grieve while others were watching? "Don't cry—be strong; don't let the weakness take over." She could still hear her mother's voice like it was in the same room, yet Delaney Evans knew her mother was hundreds of miles away—just like everyone else she knew.

Delaney sat on the stone hearth by the fireplace in the hospital waiting room. There were people everywhere, yet she had never felt more alone than she did in this moment. The tears slowly began to roll down her cheeks; she tried not to blink, but it wasn't long before she had to close her eyes. Eventually, the tears streamed down her face.

She couldn't lose him. That would kill her! Fear gripped her painfully. Riley, her son, was all she had in the world. He was her only good thing. Could she function if he were gone? Would she even want to continue? Delaney lived for that little boy. Riley depended on her. All of the sudden, Delaney realized that maybe she needed him even more then he needed her.

It had already been a long day, and Anna dreaded calling her kiddos and telling them she was going to be late yet again. Nevertheless, when working with so many church families, one never knew what could develop. She was just getting ready to head home when she received the frightened call from Tracy Cobalt that Jenny, Tracy's daughter, was in the hospital. Jenny had not been breathing well and they were all alone. Tracy pleaded with Anna to come sit with them for a while.

Anna dialed her children right away. Of course they said no problem, and promised their prayers would be sent her way. Brooke, Anna's youngest, even offered to fix ham sandwiches for her big brothers for dinner, so her mom didn't have to stress. How was she so lucky to have such a great family? Never mind luck; luck had nothing to do with it. Blessed—that's what she was! Plain and simple! Anna's husband John worked a late shift tonight, so Anna knew she should push through as quickly as she could, making sure that the Cobalt family knew they were loved and supported as little Jenny lay in the hospital.

Asthma could sure be a nasty, life-sucking pain in the butt. Seeing that sweet girl with oxygen tubes on her little face and an IV fluid bag hooked to her fragile body had almost broken Anna last time Jenny was hospitalized. At 6 years old, little Jenny should have been running and dancing. Sometimes it was hard to understand. Yet, Anna had to trust God, knowing He was in control and working things for their best!

When she walked through the hospital doors she saw Tracy Cobalt standing in the lobby. Her face was pale and drawn and Anna felt a sudden pang of guilt that she had taken the extra 10 minutes to stop at Starbucks on her way to the ER. The cup in her hand suddenly felt awkward, like a beacon for judgment. But it had already been such a long day! And that venti Americano felt like such a great idea at the time. Anna walked quickly over to Tracy and wrapped her in a hug. She could feel the shudders of small sobs escaping from Tracy. Anna spoke a quiet prayer for her friend and the sweet daughter. She knew this could be a long evening.

———————————————

Oh my goodness—so much blood.

Blake James hurriedly grabbed a white rag from the kitchen towel drawer and then immediately returned it, grabbing a brown towel instead. His mom's voice rang in his ears.
"White and blood don't mix, scares ya when you see a

towel drenched in your own blood." As he approached his little sister, he turned on the kitchen sink and rinsed her hand to see how deep the cut was. Then Blake wrapped the towel firmly around her hand. Brooke was not looking so good. She was in shock for sure. Suddenly, Blake wished his mother hadn't needed to go to the hospital tonight. Blake held his sisters hand in his own and got down on his knees in front of her. "Okay Brookey, it's gonna be okay. We'll get this bleeding stopped and figure it all out, okay?"

Brooke fell into his arms and Blake prayed a quick prayer out loud to comfort his sister.

"Hey Ben, I need you," Blake called into the next room. "Can you come here?" Blake was trying to keep his voice calm to not further upset Brooke.

"What's up?" Ben James walked into the kitchen, headphones hanging around his neck. His music blared so loudly that Blake could hear it across the room. "Hey I need my phone. Brooke cut her finger and I need to talk to Mom."

"Oh, can I see?"

"No, just get my stinkin' phone!" Ben rounded the corner and 15 seconds later came back with his brother's phone. Blake noticed he had also shut off his MP3 player. Maybe Benjamin James was capable of being serious after all. Miracles do happen.

"Okay Brookey, I'm gonna call Mom now. We got this." A little smile poked out from under the crocodile tears, and Blake mustered a deep breath and dialed the phone. As he heard his mom's voicemail box greeting, he just hung up. Knowing his mom, it would be weeks before she checked her voicemail. Texting was a much better way to go.

"I know God is in control and I know my baby is in His hands, but it all seems like too much," Tracy told Anna as they sat in the hospital room. "I really wish Mark was here. Jenny is doing so much better now. The doctor said her oxygen saturation is almost normal."

Anna felt sad for Tracy. She could not imagine being here alone without her husband. "They're gonna keep her overnight for observation. I feel safer when she is here, but what about tomorrow, what about next week? What if next time I'm not with her when she can't breathe?" Anna could feel her own tears welling as she saw the tears roll down Tracy's face. She prayed for the words, for the answer needed, but she had nothing.

Anna thought of her own sweet baby girl at home, healthy and full of life. What if it was her sweet Brooklyn lying in that bed? Anna took Tracy's hand and looked her in the eyes.

"I don't know why God does things the way He does," she stated, "but I do know this! God loves Jenny and He wants the best for your girl! And if there's anything I can do to help you, I am here! You have a whole church that loves you and we will do whatever we can!"

Anna didn't want Tracy to think her attention was wandering, but in her pocket she felt the vibrating of her phone. The wall clock said 6:40. If the kids needed her, John wouldn't be home until 10 at the earliest. She needed to get home and get Brooke to bed and make sure the kids got their homework done. Not to mention, there were piles of dishes and laundry to be washed, dried, and put away. She was at least an hour away from home if traffic was light, and heaven knew who needed her on the phone. It was time to wrap it up here. Anna felt the short beep of a text message in her pocket and thanked God she wouldn't have to take the time to listen to her voicemail. Sometimes it was the small victories that mattered. She would check it as soon as she got to her car, and could return the missed call.

Just at that perfect moment, Mark Cobalt walked in the door. Anna had never been so happy to see him. She thankfully watched relief wash over Tracy's face at his arrival. Now Anna could sleep tonight, knowing she didn't leave her sweet, stressed out friend at the hospital alone. One more hug and a final prayer with both of the Cobalts and Anna was out the door.

Delaney paced the floor. Her stomach growled, but how could she even think about eating while her baby was in an operating room, fighting for his little life? How long had he been in there? The wall clock said 6:47 p.m. Two hours and 16 minutes had passed. Didn't the doctor know she needed to hear something? Didn't he know she was going crazy?

Across the room, Delaney saw a vending machine. Maybe a bottle of water would take away this sick taste in her mouth. Was this the taste of fear? As she stood in front of the soda machine, Delaney no longer cared about who was watching or who might think she was crazy. She let the tears fall free. Her stomach tensed and devastation and fear gripped her. For a moment, she felt like she was going to pass out. She whipped around quickly to find a place to sit down and smacked into a body.

She braced herself, nearly knocking the unsuspecting woman to the ground.

After leaving little Jenny's room, Anna decided to pop by the vending machines and grab a treat for each of her kids, a peace offering of sorts. Skittles for Blake, a Pepsi for Ben, and some gummy bears for little Brooke would more than suffice. She could smell the vending machine coffee as she got closer, and decided she could definitely do without another cup of coffee tonight. Suddenly, another person ran into her, nearly knocking her over. As she fought to keep her balance, Anna James found herself staring into the face of a young girl. She looked to be about nineteen years old—if that. The girl looked even more stunned at the collision than Anna felt.

"I am so sorry! I was just—" The young lady was stumbling over her words and looked shocked. Anna took her arm and led her to a seat in the corner.

"Are you okay, sweetheart? You don't look so well."

"I'm okay," the girl answered hastily, but the truth was clear; this young lady was definitely not okay. Anna took a seat next to the girl and smiled.

"Wanna talk about it?" Anna asked. Delaney shrugged her shoulders. She had no idea who this woman was, yet when she sat down with her, Delaney felt a sudden peace.

"I am Anna James. I'm from Belfair and I'm here visiting a friend. I was just heading out, but if you need to talk, I can stay a few more minutes."

Delaney wasn't sure if it was the woman's warm smile, her soft demeanor, or something else altogether, but she started to spill her guts to this woman. Anna James was a Godsend. Something about her reminded Delaney of her pastor's wife from back home. Cindy had been so kind and so easy to talk to. With the memories still fresh and raw, Delaney began to talk. She started sharing a story of a little boy fighting for his life in an operating room just down the hall—Delaney's own son.

With her phone and the clock forgotten, Anna began to listen. Distracted completely from where she needed to be, Anna became lost in the need of this young woman. Silently, privately, she began to pray for the broken girl.

Chapter 2

Blake got Brooke settled on the couch, but her hand was still bleeding pretty badly. He was pretty sure his little sister needed to see a doctor. Blake picked up his phone again and called his grandma. She answered on the second ring and at the sound of her voice, Blake felt a bit of relief. "Hey Grandma," his words came tumbling out a hundred words a minute. "Mom is at a hospital visit. Brooke was slicing an apple and cut her finger pretty bad. What should I do? I think it might need stitches." As quickly as she had picked up the phone, June James assured her grandson that she was on her way. She told him to keep pressure on the cut and promised to be there in five minutes.

It was fortunate that June was already in town. She was dropping off some information for the upcoming ladies' retreat at a friend's house when Blake called her. June hated blood, but she sure loved her grandkids! She practically flew across town to the neighborhood where her son and daughter-in-law lived. It was 6:30 already, and June knew the clinic closed in 30 minutes. If she hurried, they would make it in time.

Blake was standing on the porch waiting for her when she pulled into the driveway. As soon as she came to a stop, Blake and Ben loaded their sister into their grandmother's SUV and they were off to Belfair's very own Harrison Urgent Care. It had been built not long ago and the James family was beyond appreciative for the new facility, which they frequented regularly.

"Thanks Grandma. What would we do without you?" Blake exclaimed emphatically. He sat next to his sister and nervously examined her hand. Little Brooke's towel had become literally saturated with blood, and suddenly Blake was very thankful for his Grandma June. And June was very thankful for the good care her sweet guys had taken of little Brooke.

Years ago when June James was given a second chance at life, she knew from that point on that family was the most important thing—next to God—in her life. June wanted to help however she could! God had given her a do-over. June would never miss the miracle in that. She would do everything she could to help in any and every situation, and she had told her kids as much. June was most definitely John and Anna's biggest fan.

Anna listened to Delaney sob and pour out her story for about 40 minutes. Anna was starting to feel a bit antsy. She knew she needed to call her kids and explain her delay. She also needed to check the message on her phone. When Delaney paused, Anna pulled out a business card with her cell number and church phone number on it. Anna explained to Delaney that she was a pastor, and that she worked with kids and families at a little church in her town. "I know that we could help you, Delaney, if you want it." Anna was completely divided; overwhelmed with split feelings of guilt for leaving this sweet girl, and knowing she had to get home to her own kids. Her children won. She was a mom. She needed to go. Delaney took Anna's card. She really did like this woman but, church, with all of its rules and fake people? She didn't need church; she was however starting to think maybe she did need a friend. -So Delaney put Anna James' card in her small diaper bag.

"I will be praying for Riley—maybe you will consider giving me a call tonight when he gets out of surgery. Just let me know that he is okay! Then when he is all better come and see me, okay? I would love to meet him." Anna continued, "But really, if nothing else, at least let me know how the surgery turns out. He must be pretty special, to have a mom who loves him like you do!"

As Anna walked to her car she took out her phone to use the flashlight. It was 7:50. If she rushed, she could still make it home in time to tuck Brooke in and maybe get the house picked up before John came home. Anna froze in the parking garage as she saw the texts from Blake in her unread messages. How had she missed the notifications?

Blake – Mom call me B cut her hand

Blake – Mom where are you Grandma is on her way FREAKING out here call me

Blake – Mom we are at urgent care B is getting stitches

Blake – CALL ME PLEASE

Anna frantically tapped out a quick message.

On my way call me

She ran to her car like someone was chasing her. Man, it was amazing how fast she could run when adrenaline kicked in. Anna set her GPS to *Home*, and booked it. What kind of mom was she? How could she have let herself get so distracted? Praise God for June. Her baby would be okay. But she was surely a horrible mother.

The rest of the way home, Anna prayed. She popped between prayers for Brooke, Jenny and Riley, and the eight-month-old baby who was fighting for his life. She also prayed God would help her to know how to navigate all the things going on in her life.

June was thrilled when, due to the blood, the nurses took Brooke back to a room almost as soon as they walked in the door. They didn't even seem upset that the James' had stormed the doors at 6:53, only seven minutes before closing. It was just a little more proof to what June always believed. There were still good people in the world!

"What do we have here? Oh, Brooklyn James, what did you do to yourself?" Dr. Tomas saw the tears begin to well. He instantly changed his tone. "I hate to see a princess in pain! We will have you fixed up in no time!" Wide-eyed, Brooke looked up at her big brother and then strained to whisper something to the doctor.

Bless Blake's heart. Brooke was scared and asked him to sit with her, and Blake James did not hesitate to climb up on the table with his sad sister and hold her while Dr. Tomas cleaned her wound and stitched her up. Brooke knew Dr. Steve Tomas very well. Their two families were great friends, and his daughter Sadie was one of Brooke's besties. Steve continuously cracked little jokes and helped her get over her fear of the small needle. Blake still had her all wrapped up in her warm blankets, and as Steve finished up, June could not be happier with the little community where they all lived! When Brooke's blood pressure was nearly normal and she was no longer feeling faint, and her heart rate lowered, Steve was ready to let them leave the clinic. He promised to call in the morning and check on his little patient. He said he would probably stop in and see the family tomorrow before his shift if John was going to be home. June agreed to relay the message, signed the paperwork, and took the prescription script from the doctor. Then they were off.

Chapter 3

Franklin T. Evans sat behind his large mahogany desk, contemplating the business empire he had built. None of it meant anything to him right now. He would give it all up just to hold her in his arms again. What had happened? Where was she? Did she know the countless tears he had shed for her? How long had it been now? Tomorrow would mark a year and a half since he had seen her face.

If Frank closed his eyes, he could see her, his ten-year-old princess, jumping into his arms after he came home from a long day at work. When she was sixteen, he remembered her getting ready for her first school dance. "Could I have this dance, my beautiful moonbeam?" He had asked her. "You will be by far the most beautiful young lady in the room. Collin won't be able to take his eyes off of you." Her face had beamed as they danced around and around in the spacious entryway of their home. Franklin's mind flashed to graduation day. Was that really only last year? She had smiled at him and said, "I'm going go to work for you someday, Dad. Then you will always have sunbeams and moonbeams at work." Where was his Moonbeam now? Where was his only child, his sun and moon?

Franklin sat up a little straighter in his leather chair, staring at the letter in his hand. He had had it for two days, yet had not found the strength to open it. There was just a feeling inside that it had to be from her. More than a feeling—he would recognize that curlicue handwriting anywhere. Frank retrieved his silver letter opener out of the top drawer of his office desk and gently slid it into the top of the cream-colored envelope. He pulled out the soft lilac-colored pages. He could smell the slightest hint of baby powder. Franklin closed his eyes and remembered holding little Delaney for the first time. She had felt so small and fragile in his arms, so sweet, so tiny. She had grown up to be such a beautiful girl. Franklin opened his eyes and began to read.

Dear Daddy,

I am so sorry. I'm sorry that I've had to leave you. I'm sorry that I had to run away, and I am sorry if I ever made you question how much you mean to me. I don't know how things got so crazy. And I don't know if I will ever find a way to explain or tell you what I've done. But I want you to know that I'm okay. I don't know why you do it Daddy, but thank you for continuing to make payments on the credit card that you gave me. I have tried to spend as little as possible but without it I do not know that I would be alive. I love you so much Daddy. Please tell Mom I love her too. I am not the same girl that left Tigard a year ago. I've grown up, Daddy. I'm stronger now. So don't worry about me. I am going to be okay. I think of you every single day. I need you to know that. Maybe, just maybe, someday I will get the courage to tell you the story. And maybe, just maybe, one day you will forgive me for all the disappointment I have brought you. My heart needed you to know that it's me, what I have done, that made me leave! It was never anything you or Mom did. You were the best father a girl could ever ask for. I miss you so much. Someday I hope I can see you again. Until then, I love you forever.

Your moonbeam,

Delaney.

He could not see through the tears streaming down his face. How could his little girl ever think that she could do anything that was unforgivable? Frank didn't understand. Had he not made his love for her clear? A simple note on Delaney's pillow the day she left, had said:

Mom & Dad, I am sorry!

I need to go now.

Please let me go.

Please don't look for me.

This is what I have to do I love you.

Delaney

Franklin's stubbornness had made him decide to let her have her way. He thought she would be home in a week, then a month. Then the first year anniversary passed, and the monthly credit card statements kept coming, and in his heart he knew she was okay. Of course he would pay the bill on the card! It was his only link to his baby girl. He knew that at her age she had a right. Getting the authorities involved would have only soiled his daughter's good name, labeling her a runaway.

There was nothing he could have done, really. What would Dolores think if she ever found out he had been paying that darn credit card all this time? Franklin hadn't known if he was doing the right thing. His heart, however, gave him no other choice. This had been the first time he ever kept anything from his wife. She had not wanted the card to be Delaney's life line, but Franklin needed to know he was not abandoning his only daughter.

He followed Delaney through the addresses of the purchases on the card. And every time he thought about her, Franklin prayed for his little girl. He was not sure the prayers actually went anywhere, but he said them nonetheless. So here he was, letter in hand, completely out of control and totally broken. With all the money he had made over the years, in the fortress he had built, the empire he ruled, it was here that the reality of his situation broke through Franklin Evans' protective wall and the grown man, sitting in his self-made fortress, began to sob.

Chapter 4

Anna James was running into Harrison Urgent Care just as her sons, daughter, and mother-in-law were walking out. She couldn't help but feel a sting of guilt about the fact that she wasn't there earlier. But stronger than that was the sense of pride she had for these amazing people in front of her. Little Brooklyn ran out and threw her arms around her mom, giant tears rolling down her face.

"I was brave, Mom, I was brave and Blake helped me, he sat up on the cushion with me and helped me not to cry! Then Ben told me if I made it through the stitches he would give me five bucks. I was brave Mom, now Ben owes me five bucks!" Brooke said matter-of-factly. Anna couldn't help but smile. Ben was forever bribing his sister. Anna was beginning to see so much of herself in Benjamin James. He just wanted to make the world happy. He always had a joke and a smile for her. She looked at both of her sons individually in their eyes and mouthed thanks. They both smiled at her, with genuine love staring back at her. How could these really be her kids? She was blessed for sure.

"I do not know how to thank you, June," said Anna, hugging her children's grandmother in a giant bear hug. "What would I do without you?" There was no look of condemnation or self-satisfaction on June James' face as she smiled at Anna. There was just sincerity.

"It's fine, sweetheart, you know what the Lord has told me. This is my job, and I am so thankful I am here to do it. Steve said he would call to check on Brooke in the morning and maybe stop by and look at the wound and see John."

"That is so great of him; it is a real blessing to have him at the clinic." As the three kids hopped in their mom's white Volvo, Anna hugged her mother-in-law again, giving her one last thank you. When they arrived at last, the James family wearily trooped through the door of their modest home. Anna looked down at the clock on the oven. How in the world was it almost 9:30? It was going to be a long night.

"Okay kiddos, everyone have a seat in the living room." The kids shuffled in and sat down on top of the laundry mounds and comforters still left piled on the couch from the morning. "I am so proud of you all. You guys handled this situation like champs! I'm sorry I wasn't here to take care of it, but I really am proud of you. I love you guys so much and Brooke, you were so brave ... but maybe we should take a break from knives when mommy's not home!" Brooke smiled up at her mom, nodding with big eyes in total agreement. Anna continued,

"All right guys, it's 9:30 and definitely time to head to bed. You lucky ducks are going to get away with no chores tonight. Mom will take care of it."

The kids shuffled off to bed with hugs and kisses and a couple songs played on the piano. Anna took a moment to linger at the piano after the kids were tucked in, and she began to play and sing.

When peace, like a river, attendeth my way,

When sorrows like sea billows roll;

Whatever my lot, Thou has taught me to say,

It is well, it is well, with my soul.

It is well, with my soul,

It is well, with my soul,

It is well, it is well, with my soul.

With one last deep breath and 20 minutes remaining before John would be home, Anna got up and began to tidy the house. She made John a frozen pizza for dinner and packed tomorrow's lunches for everyone. As she was putting the last of the freshly washed mugs away in the cupboard, she heard

Blake's voice behind her say, "I love you, Mom." Anna turned around and embraced her son in a big hug.

"Thank you for all you did today, Blake. I don't know what I would have done without you."

"No problem, I was glad to help. But Mom, it sure would be nice to have you around a little more. I got a little scared when you didn't respond to my messages."

"I am sorry Blake. I really am. I'll work on that, okay buddy?" Anna said. "It was a crazy situation with the Cobalts in the hospital. I need to come up with a better system for checking messages."

"How about leaving the ringer on, or occasionally checking a voicemail?" Blake suggested with a little smirk.

"Yeah, yeah, whatever," Anna scoffed humorously. "Now off to bed with you. You're hard enough to get up in the morning as it is!" She laughed.

"Yeah," Blake answered with a smile, "I do need my beauty sleep." Anna chuckled and smacked his behind, and with a huff Blake headed off to bed.

Chapter 5

It all started when Riley began having a hard time breathing while he was nursing. At first, Delaney thought the little guy must have a cold. Then she noticed that he always seemed to be breathing quite rapidly. His breathing was labored, and at times his skin started to look as if it were turning a pale gray.

Delaney was scared, but she knew Riley needed to see a doctor. Delaney had been very careful about how she used the cash she had left, and she knew her dad would figure things out if doctor bills showed up on his credit card. The words *congenital heart disease* were the scariest words that Delaney had ever heard. Congenital heart disease, or CHD, as the doctor called it, was a type of heart disease that children were born with. Riley's had caused heart defects that were probably present at birth. The doctor explained to Delaney that only about 1% of babies born each year in the United States has CHD.

In Riley's case, they suspected that he had a heart valve disorder—a narrowing of his aortic valve, which restricted blood flow. They made an appointment two days later with Dr. Winters, a children's heart surgeon at Tacoma Children's Hospital. Dr. Winters told her that heart surgery would be Riley's only chance. Now here she sat, while they cut open her precious baby. They had warned her it could take several hours. Delaney was scared and needed to hear something. Delaney thought back to the days when she didn't have to do hard things alone. Man, she missed her parents, she missed her friends, and Delaney sure missed Collin.

Delaney sunk deeper into her sadness with every hour that passed. Fear gripped her heart as if the feeling had grown talons. That strange woman she met had talked about the peace of God; she had talked about the healing power of God. Was God really there for her? Did He really care about her? Delaney closed her eyes and bowed her head. "God, if you are really there, and if you really love me and Riley, please heal my baby. God, if you heal my baby maybe I'll even give you another chance. God, if you fix Riley's heart I will go to church, I promise. Amen."

As she opened her eyes, she saw Dr. Winters walking into the waiting room. Delaney stood up and walked over to her, tears streaming down her face. The lines of Dr. Winters' mouth curved up into an almost smile as she told Delaney that Riley had made it through the surgery just fine. Within the hour, someone would come out to get her and she would be able to see her baby boy. Delaney fell to her knees and begin to cry, and under her breath she whispered, "Thank you!" to a God she desperately wanted to believe in. But maybe, just maybe, this was a sign that God loved her after all. And as soon as possible, Delaney wanted to find a church.

Delaney picked up her cell and typed in the number on the card Anna James gave her. She hesitated to hit *Send*; it was almost 10 o'clock at night. Anna had said to call. Surely, she had known it would be late. The woman picked up on the second ring. The conversation was not long, but Anna's voice was so kind. She seemed genuinely relieved to hear that Riley made it through the hard part. Crazy how this women Delaney had never met before could seem to actually care. She had appeared to feel her sorrow at the hospital today, and then have compassion for her status and a regard for her and Riley's well-being. Delaney could only remember that kind of compassion from one other person in her life, Grandma Ginny. Delaney suddenly remembered one afternoon sitting with her grandma after school during a piano lesson. Her grandma told her a story about a young lady that went to her BSF Women's Bible Study Fellowship group. She remembered the story of a girl who had joined the group when she had met her grandmother and seen something different in her.

Delaney suddenly wondered if Church and God were not the real problem with religion, but instead maybe there were just people who claimed to be Christians that really had no clue what that meant. This was so foreign to Delaney, yet she felt the need to look deeper into things. "Still trying to teach me about Jesus aren't you grandma even now that you are gone." Delaney whispered to no one. Yes she would most definitely be heading to church, very soon.

Chapter 6

Wednesday nights were a bit crazy for the James family. Each person headed different directions after school, until they all met together at the church for kid's theater practice. Anna loved directing these local kids as they used their talents for the Lord. But some weeks were easier than others. Tonight had been one of the more trying of nights. Only three of the twenty-four kids had remembered their scripts. Two of the costumes that she had made did not fit the students they were supposed to fit, and three of the teenage helpers on the team had simply decided to not show up.

Anna sent Blake into the office to copy some extra scripts, while Anna explained to the affected children about their ill-fitting costumes. She would get Lauren to fix them so they would be done right this time. Suddenly, Anna wished she had asked Lauren to do the costumes in the first place. Lauren had had so much on her plate with her mother's illness that Anna had not wanted to bug her. Sue was home from the hospital now, though, and doing so much better. Anna's back was killing her, and she was starting to get a headache. But . . . *the show must go on!*

Solid Rock Musical Theater only had four more practices before performance day, and there was no way Anna was going to let silly little things like this get in her way. Blake burst through the doors with the scripts and as Anna took them and began to give them to the kids in need, she lectured them about how they should all have their lines memorized by now.

"Next week, no scripts!" Anna barked. Ben replied, "Well, if you would take ten minutes with me to run through my lines, maybe I wouldn't need this!" Anna felt a sting of guilt as she thought about how little time she had spent with her kids this week, yet that attitude was not going to fly!

"We will talk about that when we get home." Ben looked down, knowing he was in for a lecture. But Anna saw the glare in his eyes that said he was not happy with the situation. Ben knew he had to somehow let go of this hot headed, angry thing that was happening to him lately. But how do you explain to your mom that you just feel angry all the time these days? Ben was frustrated that his mom seemed to have time for everyone else's problems, but didn't even seem to see him. Ben felt like he was invisible to Anna James. The only time he got her attention was when he mouthed off. Ben knew this was not the kind of attention he wanted from his mom, but he was unsure how to get what he wanted.

"Okay, places everyone," Anna said loudly above the bustle of noise in the room. The lights came up on the stage and the kids took their places. Anna smiled as she spotted sweet little Jenny on stage holding her big sister Beth's hand. It was hard to believe it was just last week that Jenny was close to death, lying in a hospital bed.

Brooke and Ben began the second scene with a song about keeping your eyes on Jesus, and Anna couldn't help but smile at the way her children sounded. They were growing up so fast. If Anna didn't slow things down a bit, she was going to miss it. She needed to talk to John about getting away soon. Maybe it was time for a beach trip. Truly, the only way to get a break around here was to go away. If you were in town, you were on call. That was all there was to it. Yep, it was definitely time to get away. Hopefully it could somehow be worked into her family's budget. Anna would figure it out. God always had a way of providing for her family their wants and their needs.

Anna spoke a quiet prayer that God would give her the insight to see what Ben needed. He really was not his chipper self lately. He seemed distant, always frustrated, short fused, irritable. *Lord help me fight for him the right way. I don't want*

*him to lose sight of how much he is loved, by me, and
even more Lord, by you.*

Little Riley was sitting up and almost ready
to leave the hospital. Delaney was sitting in the
corner filling out paperwork for financial assistance
to pay these hospital bills. Delaney didn't even
know what address to have the bills sent to. How
was she going to do this? Riley needed a home. She
was tired of popping around from cheap hotel to
cheap hotel. Delaney was sure the boy must be a bit
hungry. Delaney reached over the rolling table and
grabbed the little boy crackers. As she handed
them to him, his smile lit up and his eyes shone
with life. Suddenly Delaney felt gratitude once again
for Dr. Winters and the team of physicians that had
saved her baby. Delaney's mind wandered to her
parents. She missed them so much. What would
her parents think if they knew the situation? They
would be disgusted by her! She was pretty sure of
that. They would be so disappointed. He father had
had so many dreams for her. She had not fulfilled
even one.

Delaney had lost at least ten pounds since
she left last year. Her hair was longer and definitely
needed to be cut. Her nails were chipped and her
clothes were worn, but all of her money had gone to

Riley, and how do you get a haircut with a baby in your arms anyway? Delaney was very adamant about always keeping Riley within her sights.

There were so many times Delaney wished she could drop her son off with her parents. That, however, would never be possible. They didn't even know Riley existed. They would just love little Riley. Her mother would smother him in kisses and her dad would throw him in the air and catch him and he would giggle. He would, that is, if all this had happened under different circumstances. Riley was sure missing out, not getting to know Franklin and Dolores Evans. She often wondered if she had made the right choice in leaving. Her parents were loving and kind. However, she would only have to take a moment and think about the maybes, think about how things could have gone wrong. Then she knew she had done what she had to do. As much as Delaney regretted her life choices, she did not ever regret Riley. He was an angel. He saved her when she hadn't even known she needed saving. She had a job, a duty, and a responsibility to protect her little angel.

Delaney's mind filled with an image of her father. One day she had come home from practice very upset. One of the girls on her squad had played a prank on her that resulted in her getting sick and throwing up all over the school gym floor. Sarah Thompson had put ipecac in two of the girls' water bottles after finding out they had narked on her for drinking at the football game the previous Friday. Sarah then proceeded to tell the coach that Delaney had been drinking and was now sick from it! Delaney remembered her father picking her up from school while she was still violently ill. She remembered telling her dad she had never ever drunk alcohol and that there was something out of place. Delaney remembered her father wrapping her in his arm and telling her he believed her. He said he would get to the bottom of what happened.

Delaney could still feel his arms, smell his after shave, and hear his words as he told her she was his baby, his moonbeam and it was his job to make sure she was protected. Her dad worked hard and got to the bottom of the story. He had protected her. And that is essentially what Delaney was doing for Riley. He was her responsibility. "I miss you daddy . . . I wish there could have been another way," she whispered to herself. Now, somehow, she needed to figure this all out. Riley was counting on her. She was not going to let him down. If only she knew how she was going to accomplish the next step of their lives. But one thing was certain: she would do whatever she had to do to take care of her baby—even if it meant she had to contact her father.

Chapter 7

Jessica Winters stepped into the shower and let the hot water pour over the back of her shoulders. Jessica had never been one to bring her patients' troubles home with her! Yet, there was something about Delaney Evans. Maybe it was the innocence in her eyes, or the way her sadness seemed to saturate the room. Maybe the truth was, she reminded her of her own Hailey. It seemed the more she tried not to think about the girl, the more God brought her to mind. Jessica knew exactly what she needed to do. She toweled off, got dressed, and fed Mittens, the white-pawed black cat. Jessica threw her breakfast dishes into the sink and grabbed her purse. When was the last time she couldn't wait to get back to work? It had been long ago. She didn't know what it was, but Jessica Winters knew there was so much more to Delaney Evans' story and she was determined to figure out the whole picture behind that sweet young face. With new purpose and a spring to her step, Jessica was off to work.

"Earth to Anna," John came up behind her and wrapped his arms around her waist. "What's got you all spacey?"

"I don't know, just a lot on my mind I guess"

"Like what?" John said taking Anna's hand and leading her over to the couch. "I don't know. Life, I guess. I am just wondering if one day I am going to look back at my life and regret my choices."

"Wow, those are some deep thoughts." Anna smiled over at her husband.

"I know they are. I am a deep person!" She said with a laugh. "Don't get me wrong; I love what I do. I just think I need to work a little harder to let the kids know they are my number one priority."

"Hmm, I don't know if I like the sound of that," John said, pulling Anna halfway onto his lap. "I think I am gonna need to be your number one priority."

"Yeah, yeah, yeah," Anna smiled, tilting her head down to kiss her husband.

"Dude, get a room, you two!" Benjamin exclaimed as he walked into the room with a fake grimace, hiding his underlying smile.

"We will continue this later," John spoke softly into her ear, his murmurings giving her goose bumps.

"Until later," she whispered back.

Anna loved lazy Saturdays. All of her loves were under the same roof for at least part of the day. Saturday morning breakfast was high on the list of Anna's favorite things.

"Morning Ben, wanna make the eggs for me and I will do the bacon? Dad has kindly volunteered to do the pancakes."

"Sure," Ben answered, walking into the kitchen and pulling out the electric skillet from under the cupboard.

"I will make the toast," Brooke added, as she pushed the small red stool over to the fridge so she could snatch the loaf of bread from its lofty perch.

"Perfect!" Anna told her with a wink. "It will be a team effort."

"Team James is my favorite team," Brooke remarked with a smile.

"You are so corny, Brooke," needled Ben.

"Whatever, meanie," she retorted, sticking her tongue out at her brother.

"Okay, don't even start, you two! Is your brother awake yet?" John asked Ben. Ben shrugged his shoulders.

"I would gladly be the one to wake him if you want me to." Ben held up a big glass of water.

"Let's let Dad take care of this one," Anna said with a laugh in her voice. "It is safer for everyone that way. You have eggs to perfect!"

Ben's smile lit up his face. "You're no fun at all."

"Yes, I think we have already established this ... my lack of merrymaking. Deal with it!"

When the food was served, everyone gathered around the table to eat. Ben sat the big bowl of eggs on the table and Blake gladly heaped a jumbo size portion onto his plate.

"Save some for the rest of us," John said as he poured some OJ into his glass.

"That is why I made all 18 eggs," Ben said. "My eggs are irresistible."

"Are they now," John reached to ruffle Ben's curly red hair. "They are pretty good."

They all ate their fill. The table was full of smiles and stories, jokes and silly anecdotes. In that moment, Anna's heart was full. John met Anna's gaze and gave her a knowing look.

It is well with my soul, Anna thought. With his eyes, John seemed to tell her heart that even on days when things were rocky, the James family was going to be okay! They always were.

Delaney sat in stony silence as she read the card that had appeared on the stainless steel table tray over Riley's bed. She closed her eyes and read the words again.

Delaney Evans,

This letter is to inform you that your doctor bill and hospital stay have been paid in full. The donor would like to remain anonymous, but asked me to share with you the reason they chose to take the burden off your hands. They feel that the Lord told them too. All they want in return is for you to consider the amazing love that God has for you and your sweet son. You should also know a donation has been made to cover Riley Evans' follow up care at our Belfair clinic.

Information attached.

God bless you.

Dr. Winters

P.S. If you have any further concerns, please feel free to give me a call. My number is on the card attached as well.

Delaney sat frozen. They only thing that moved were the stunned tears rolling down her stiff cheeks. Delaney shook from her stupor and looked down at Riley's sleeping form. *Okay, God, I'm listening,* she thought. Did things like this really happen? Delaney had had no idea how she was going to pay the thousands of dollars accumulated for Riley's care, but this was too much. She needed to speak with Dr. Winters; maybe the woman could give her the answers her swimming mind needed. In a fog, Delaney walked from her son's room in search of the good doctor.

Chapter 8

Collin Haggerty sat on his dorm bed, more than ready for Christmas vacation. He wasn't sure, however, if he was ready to head home. Everything in his home town still reminded him of Delaney. When was he going to let her go? She was obviously gone. It had been more than a year, but he thought about her way more than he should. The only other thing he really missed was seeing his sister Cara. He was still working to repair the damage he had done in neglecting her during his time of depression after Delaney left. Home—it just seemed like a sad, broken place.

When Collin had first heard that his buddies were taking a dirt biking trip the first week of Christmas break, it had sounded like a wonderful idea. Collin used to spend a lot of time on a bike back in high school at his friend Jax's house.

Jax's parents ran a paint ball park in Sherwood. During the off hours, Jax was often allowed to have friends over to ride dirt bikes and ATVs all over their vast property. Last week he had texted Jax to see if he wanted to drive up to Washington and ride, camp, and hang out for the week. He could hardly wait to reconnect with his old friend. Jax and Collin went way back. They had played football and lacrosse together at Jesuit High

School, and Jax had been the one who introduced Collin to Pastor Roy at Rock Creek Community Church.

There had always been something different and magnetic about Jax and his family. It didn't take long for Collin to figure out that it was Jesus. Jax's religion was different from many of the other kids' that Collin knew; it was more like a relationship with Christ, Jax would say. Whatever it was, it was different.

It wasn't until after Delaney disappeared that Collin really began to make changes in his own way of thinking. He was completely broken after she left. Collin didn't know what he would have done without God and Pastor Roy. Things were pretty dark in his world. There were times when Collin really wanted to just end it all. He even tried once. Praise God he had not succeeded. Collin's parents wanted to help him, but they just didn't know what he needed. They sent him to a counselor and tried to buy him things, but that didn't help. Collin jumped into Jesus with both feet. He would never look back! He was finally starting to feel like he could do this life thing again.

When Collin shared with Roy that he felt like God was calling him into ministry with teens, Roy took Collin to a Northwest Friday at Northwest

University. At the visit to the school, Collin got to see the campus, meet a few professors, sleep in a dorm room, and attend a chapel service. NU was Pastor Roy's alma mater. Collin decided to give up his dad's dreams of him becoming a future Harvard law student, for a call to ministry. Collin knew his parents were still hoping NU was a passing phase. Collin didn't think he would be happy anywhere else! His parents would accept it eventually, he hoped. Until they did, he would push through and try to become the man he believed God was calling him to be.

Often he still wondered about Delaney. He wondered where she was and why she ran away. Collin had finally come to the place where he accepted that she was gone and he did not have the ability to figure it all out. So every day he gave it back to the Lord and prayed not only that Delaney was safe, but that wherever she was, she would encounter God

Delaney saw Dr. Winters standing at the door of the room across from Riley's, holding a clipboard. Delaney walked slowly to her, contemplating what she was going to say. Bewildered, she just stood there until the doctor looked up at her.

"Can I help you?" She asked. Delaney just stood there staring, dumbstruck. Dr. Winters smiled. "I know you are probably a little shocked right now, but what's done is done. I hope you can just see it as a blessing." Delaney continued to stare. "All right, sweetheart," Dr. Winters put her hand on Delaney's shoulder. "I am nearly done with my rounds and you and Riley are last on my list. I know he is being released tonight and I am wondering if you guys have a ride home." Jessica Winters had noticed right away that there was no record of a physical address for Riley and Delaney anywhere in their documents.

Delaney was silent for a minute, wondering what she should say. "We don't actually have a home . . . um . . . well . . . we are living out of the car I got for graduation."

Neither of these things seemed appropriate, and after the last year of being so careful about whom she talked to and what she said, Delaney could not believe she was contemplating honesty with this woman. Jessica Winters said a short prayer under her breath. *Give me the words, Lord.*

"How far from the hospital do you live?" Dr. Winters asked.

"Actually I don't know. I have my car, but I am not really sure where we are headed from here."

"Can I ask you a really personal question, Ms. Evans? Do you have a home to go home to?"

Tears began to pour out of Delaney's eyes yet again as she simply shook her head, *no*. Delaney was overcome with the deepest, most overwhelming feeling she had ever felt. She was trembling now! Jessica prayed under her breath again and said words she had never, ever said to a patient before. Throwing all caution to the wind, and all sanity as well, for that matter, Jessica asked, "Delaney, would you like to come stay the night with me while you figure out what you are going to do?" Delaney was about to say thanks, but no thanks, when Dr. Winters spoke up again. "Riley is still very fragile. He may still need medical care, and a warm place to sleep would definitely be a plus."

Delaney looked at Dr. Winters through narrowed eyes and asked, "Why? Why are you helping us? Why did someone pay our bill? Why would anyone even care about us?"

"Because Jesus loves you, Delaney, and sometimes He uses others to show you that. What do you say? I will be done here in about an hour.

Why don't you go get things ready to go and let's go make that little boy a comfy area to finish his recovery. Deal?"

With a lack of conviction in her voice, Delaney repeated the doctor's word back at her. "Deal." As the doctor turned and walked away, Delaney's tears again began to cascade down her face. What in the world was going on here? *Okay God, I am listening*, she thought.

Jessica headed to her office to make a few phone calls. She was going to need a little help with this one. And she knew just who to call. Anna James would know what to do.

As Dr. Winters walked away Delaney began to cry in earnest. She was no longer crying because she was afraid, God had saved Riley. No she cried because for the first in a long time Delaney felt hope. Maybe just maybe God didn't hate her after all.▯

Chapter 9

Collin's trip to Belfair was filled with fun conversation and catching up with his old friend. The trip took about two hours and there was not even one minute of quiet while they drove. They blared old '80s rock ballads while Jax told Collin about his last year at Portland State University.

"Any new ladies in your world?" Jax asked Collin with a smile on his face that didn't quite reach his eyes.

"I may have sworn off women forever," Collin said with a sigh.

"Not over her yet, huh?"

"Nope, definitely not," Collin answered. When they arrived at Belfair State Park, they met up with Collin's other friend from school. Jax had brought up three bikes—one for Collin, one for himself, and one for Jamie, another kid from NU who had a bike back in his home town of Butte, Montana, but had had no way of getting it to the party.

"Hey, thanks man for sharing the wealth. I couldn't have come if it weren't for you, man," said Jamie.

"My pleasure," said Jax, "I'm glad it worked out. Any friend of Collin's is a friend of mine." That night the guys sat around the campfire roasting marshmallows, and Jamie played some worship music on his guitar while the other guys sang.

"I really needed this guys! Thanks again for letting me tag along!" exclaimed Jamie.

"Yeah, things are not quite so inspirational back in Portland either," added Jax. "Hey, I didn't have time to run to the auto parts store back home before we left. I want to pick up a can of fix-a-flat before we head out to Tahuya tomorrow. Is that cool?" There was a round of *no worries* and *that's cools* around the circle. It was getting late and the boys wanted to get a decent start for the day tomorrow, so they headed to their tents to rest up.

When Anna got Jessica's urgent call for baby items, Anna got right to work. With a couple of phone calls and a quick run to Wal-Mart, she was able to get the things purchased, picked up, and dropped off at Jessica's house in plenty of time. John helped her pull it all together, and now, thanks to Jessica's hide-a-key, they were even able to get in and get it all set up before Jess and her guest got there. After the conversation with Jess, Anna was absolutely certain that this was the same Delaney that she had met at the children's hospital. As John put the portable crib in the corner of the room, Anna laid out six little boy outfits on the dresser. She filled one of the spare room drawers with diapers and wipes and another with diaper ointment, baby lotion, and other baby grooming needs. She laid out two receiving blankets inside the little bed and unfolded a super soft mini afghan that had been donated by her friend Lilly when she had heard about the need. All of the blankets Lilly made were saturated in prayer as she crocheted them, stitch by stitch. So when Anna spread the baby-sized afghan in the crib, she whispered a prayer as well. Not only for little Riley's health, but for Delaney's salvation. The final touch was a basket of goodies for Delaney that her friend Sheila had put together. On the handle was a cutout decorated letter *D* with the name *Delaney* written down the side in perfect penmanship—Sheila's signature move. The basket was filled with lotion, shampoo, conditioner, bubble bath, a scented candle, and even a box of tea and a beautiful teacup.

"The poor girl needs to feel spoiled," Sheila has said on the phone. Their little Belfair church had some of the greatest people. As she and John finished up the final details and rushed out of Jessica's house and headed home, Anna felt a sense of anticipation to see the sweet young mom again. Yet Anna couldn't help but wonder about Delaney's story. Anna was sure it was complicated. Even so, Anna prayed that she would somehow be able to make a difference in this wayward girl's life.

Dr. Winter's house was beautiful. Not huge, but plenty big enough. The best thing about it was the beautiful view. The house sat right on the canal on Belfair's southern shore. The whole front of the house on the water side was made of glass. Delaney and Riley had a nice little room all to themselves, complete with a sliding glass door that opened to a balcony facing the water. Dr. Winters, or Jessica, as she had told Delaney to call her, had even asked a friend of hers from church to drop off a pack 'n' play bed for Riley to rest in and all sorts of other baby needs! It seemed like a lot to accomplish in one night. Yet, it was like a dream. It really had been a long time since Delaney felt any sense of safety or comfort. Well, about a year and a half. Not since the day she left her parents beautiful Tigard home. Something about Jessica's home felt safe.

There was also a tinge of something a little bit sad here, but Delaney couldn't put her finger on it. She was so thankful to be here. Riley could get better here. Delaney touched the lovely basket of wonderful things sitting on her dresser. It was amazingly filled with many of her favorite things. How had someone known that she loved the smell of blackberries and vanilla, or how a cup of tea at the end of a long day could relax her? Delaney was overwhelmed with what she walked into.

On the car ride to Jessica's house, the doctor had talked to Delaney about some work she needed done, like light house cleaning and cooking of meals. Jessica told Delaney that as a heart surgeon, she often had very little time to get things done. The doctor offered Delaney room and board if she would do the work needing to be done. It all sounded too good to be true. Jessica also invited her to come to church with her that Sunday— tomorrow, actually, and there was no way Delaney could refuse after everything that Jessica was doing for her. Things were looking up. Delaney was determined to be the best she could be for Dr. Winters and for Riley.

What was she going to wear? Delaney did not have a single thing that was church-worthy. Maybe she should just tell Jessica that next week would be a better time to start this church thing. As if she read her mind, Jessica knocked at the door just then.

"Do you need anything kiddo? We have about 45 minutes until we leave." Delaney walked over and opened the door. "Jessica, maybe I should wait a week before I go to church. I seriously have nothing to wear. I would be so embarrassed, and I am sure I would not want to embarrass you with my threadbare appearance. I will find some kind of odd job and get some cash to get something appropriate."

"Well, don't worry about me, sweetheart, and the Lord doesn't care what you wear. But, let me go check something. I may have a solution. What are you, about a size six?"

Walking away from the door, Jessica felt a small twinge of dread come over her. She opened the door that led down the staircase into her small basement room. Jessica pulled out a hot pink bin and lugged it up the stairs. She couldn't bring herself to open the bin. It didn't matter; she knew exactly what was in there: it was a box full of both painful memories and good memories. It was a box full of the memories of her only daughter—the daughter that left her nearly two years ago to be with Jesus. Jessica hauled the bin up the stairs, forced a smile on her face, and walked into Delaney's open room.

"I have this box of clothes I do not need anymore, and I think they are just your size. Why don't you look through it and see if there is anything that works? You can keep anything that fits."

It was like Christmas. The clothes were very nice, beautiful things, all her size. There were pants, skirts, sweaters and jackets, soft silky tops, and even a cute pair of boots. She put together an outfit quickly and walked out to say thanks to Jessica. For a split second, something like pain seemed to cross Jessica's face. It was gone as quickly as it came. "Okay," Jessica declared spiritedly, "let's do this thing. Off to church we go!" Delaney picked up Riley and followed Jessica out the door.

Collin pulled into the parking lot of O'Reilly Auto Parts Store and quickly ran up to the door, which was still locked. It looked like there was about five minutes before the door opened. Collin turned around and was headed back to sit in his car for another minute when he saw across the street something very shocking.

Collin was sure as the day that Delaney Evans was standing in the parking lot of the local church! Collin began to walk across the O'Reilly's parking lot. He would have thought he was crazy, but his Laney was standing right beside a silver 2014 Jeep Liberty. It was the car her father had gotten her for graduation in what seemed like an eternity ago.

Collin walked slowly, staring across the main road into the church parking lot across the street. He stood there dumbfounded as he saw Delaney pick up a small boy from the back seat of the car. A baby—how in the world? Delaney had a baby? Collin felt nauseous as the realization washed over him. Standing in that parking lot was the lost love of his life, and snuggled there in her arms was the very reason she was lost. Delaney had gotten pregnant. She had a baby. *He* had a baby. Collin turned around and went back to his car. Suddenly, everything made so much more sense.

It had only been that one time. They had both had too much to drink. Before that day, Collin and Laney had decided they were not ready for that in their relationship. Delaney had made a big promise to her father that she would wait. Save herself for her wedding night. But on that night, Collin could remember telling her that he loved her and that he was going to be the man she married. Delaney bought it hook, line, and sinker. And they had gone back to Laney's house. Her parents were out of town on business and Laney was supposed to be staying at a friend's house. It was about five weeks later that Delaney just disappeared. Collin had not only ruined Delaney's hope of living up to her dad's expectations that night, but they had not used any protection.

Collin got back into his car and left, running away to the camp ground. He was a coward. He did not have the guts to face her. She was the one girl he loved, and with a series of bad choices, in one night he had ruined her life forever.

Chapter 10

Surely Delaney was seeing things. Yes, that had looked like Collin's car driving by the church that morning, but there was no way. Collin was off at Harvard, or possibly home for Christmas break, but definitely not in some hole in the wall Hood Canal town just over three weeks before Christmas. Delaney grabbed little Riley tightly and headed into the church.

As Delaney walked into the building, she smelled the wonderful aroma of coffee coming from the espresso stand in the lobby. Delaney made a mental note to check it out after she touched bases with Jessica. Coffee was a luxury she had left in Oregon when she had fled. Money was tight. She refused to spend her dad's hard-earned money on frivolous things! Delaney's memory momentarily wandered back to Collin. She had loved to stop by Dutch Brothers with him on their way to school several days a week. "Caramel latte for me and a skinny vanilla latte for the most beautiful girl I know!" She could still hear him say the words. She always thought it was so cheesy. Man, what she would do to have him back!

With a shake of her head, Delaney cleared those dangerous thoughts from her mind! Collin would hate her now. Hate her for leaving, hate her for having a baby. She was screwed up. Mr. Haggerty, Collin's dad, would never allow the pretty princess to ruin Collin's perfect future. No, Collin would go to law school and take his rightful place at Haggerty & Reems. She could not entertain such thoughts of Collin holding her in his arms, promising to love her forever. Those thoughts led to hope and hope led to disappointment. Delaney already had her share of that.

Delaney quickly caught up to Jessica. They had taken two cars to church because Jessica had a shift at the hospital right after service. Delaney looked around the room. It was a nice church; the people seemed really friendly. Jessica walked Delaney to the nursery, showing her where she could take Riley if she wanted, but had also cautioned her that she might want to keep Riley with her for a couple more weeks while he finished healing and building up his little immune system. Delaney was more than relieved to keep her baby with her.

Riley was sweet as can be, sleeping through most of the service. The pastor spoke on being adopted into the family of God. He spoke of grace, forgiveness, and deep love. Delaney wanted these things.

Delaney thought about youth group back in high school, how she had gone week after week because it was often the only time she had to spend with Collin. It had never really sunk in for her though until now! Maybe now she needed it more! When the pastor ended his message with an invitation to come up and receive prayer, before she knew it, Delaney was on her feet with Jessica following right behind her. It was time to make things real with God. No longer could His existence nor His obvious care for her and Riley be ignored.

Chapter 11

After service was over, Anna hurried to finish up her obligations on the kids' end. Wreath sales were in full swing and today was the last day that people could preorder wreaths for their doors. Stacy, Anna's resident wreath maker and dear friend, was waiting for a check from Jessica, who always ordered the largest nautical wreath mixed with red and blue Poinsettia leaves. It sounded like a crazy concoction, but Stacy made it look amazing.

Anna walked over and thanked Stacy for helping the student theater kids with this fundraiser. Anna's heart went out to Stacy. Last year had been a hard one, after finding out that her husband of 15 years was having a torrid affair. Joe left her high and dry, but Stacy was a fighter. She struggled to make her own ends meet, yet still always found it in her heart to help the kids make their fundraising goal. Anna was blessed to have her as a friend.

She helped Stacy take her stuff out to her truck and then walked back into the lobby. When she saw Blake and Ben in the hallway, she called them over and had them hang out with the last three kids in the room, and then Anna booked it over to the main lobby. She had not meant to take so long with the wreath sales and was hoping to catch Delaney before she left. John was off work today, which was a special treat, and was taking Blake and Ben out riding somewhere up Elfendahl Pass. Brooke was headed over to her friend Sadie's house for the afternoon.

Anna was excited to see if her young new friend was up for lunch. Anna saw Delaney talking to Jesse Harris near the front doors. Anna approached the two and could hear Jesse asking Delaney if she wanted to go to lunch and a movie.

"I am sure my mom will watch your kid so we can go," he assured her. Delaney looked a bit pale and Anna saw this as her cue.

"Hey Delaney, are you ready for lunch?" Anna asked as she got closer. Delaney had only the shortest moment of confusion before she looked at Jesse and told him sorry, she already had plans for the day.

Anna took Delaney's arm and pulled her towards the ladies' restroom. Once inside, Anna couldn't help but giggle a little.

"Jesse is harmless. He just thinks you're pretty and jumps quick at what he likes," Anna told her new friend. "You are going to have to come up with an imaginary boyfriend to send him off the scent."

"He freaked me out," Delaney said with a timid smile. "Most of the time, the babe in arms is enough to scare the guys away."

Anna laughed. "Well, Jesse Harris doesn't scare off that easy. He is the middle of eight brothers and sisters, including two sets of twins. He likes kids." Changing the subject, Anna returned to her original mission. "So, what do you say? I have found myself alone for the afternoon. Want to get some lunch, my treat?"

"I would love to," Delaney said appreciatively, "Thank you!" The two of them exited the restroom. Anna saw John a few feet away trying to corral the boys.

"Okay John, I am off. I will see you guys in a few hours, have fun! What time do you think you will be home?"

"We're gonna ride for a couple hours, but don't worry. We won't be late. It is cold out there despite the sun, and Blake is cold blooded so we will be home for dinner by five—probably sooner." John leaned over and gave Anna a kiss. "See you tonight," he said, winking at her, then headed back the other way to find the boys.

Brooklyn ran up behind Anna and attempted to scare her. After pretending fear, Anna hugged

68

her baby girl and told her, "Have fun with Sadie. I will be there to pick you up at four, okay?"

"Okay!" Brooke answered. The little girl ran off to her friend's car and got in the back seat. Anna gave a quick wave to Sadie's mom Elaina and turned back to Delaney.

"Okay, where to?" Anna asked.

"What's good around here?" Delaney replied.

"I know just the place," Anna said.

"Sounds good, I will follow you." Buckling Riley into his car seat, Delaney thought about how great it was to feel like she had a friend again, even if her new friends all seemed to be twice her age.

———————————

Collin spent the morning trying to pretend like nothing was askew in his world. Had his eyes been playing tricks on him? Was he seeing only what he wanted to see? Did his mind miss Delaney so much that he could conjure up her image out of nowhere? Collin could smell the BBQ, he could hear the sound of the sizzling steaks, yet he had completely lost his appetite. Why didn't he stop? Why had he not investigated? Collin could be a father. He could have a child out there that he knew nothing about. The question burned inside him. He could have had answers, yet he ran in fear. Collin needed to get away from this camp site. Maybe his friends wouldn't notice there was a problem.

Anna and Delaney headed out to eat at a funny little restaurant down by the northern shore of the Canal. Anna told Delaney that it was one of her favorite places. Eclectic décor dating back to older days, farm animal figurines, and pictures took up every corner of the room. They both ate delicious prime rib dips and fat crunchy fries.

Little Riley downed at least ten fries himself. At lunch, Anna prayed Delaney would feel comfortable. Anna could tell there was a lot more going on in Delaney's world than she was letting on. On the one hand, Anna didn't want to pry, but on the other hand, there was something very intriguing about this young girl. Anna saw strength in her that mingled with insecurity and pain— definitely pain.

Collin ended up at the entrance of the park where there was a playground. It was a relatively nice day. The sun was shining, yet definitely missing warmth. December was not the warmest time of year in Western Washington along the Hood Canal. There were only a small handful of kids playing on the structure that overlooked the water. Seagulls flew over the stony beach crying their cries as if to commiserate with his melancholy mood. Collin saw a young mom pushing her child on the swing and a father helping his daughter across the monkey bars. *What kind of dad would I be?* Collin thought as he watched them. He moved slightly out of view of the playground and took a bench under the trees. Then he bowed his head for the first time all day.

"Dear Lord, I can't get this out of my head. Did I see Delaney today, or am I crazy? And if I did, Lord, how would I ever find her again? What are you trying tell me? Lord, when I headed to NU I thought I heard your voice. How could I have missed it? It has sure seemed that my steps were ordered by you. God, you even handled my father. And that was nothing short of a miracle. Lord, if I am a father, I want to do the right thing. You know I love Delaney more than I have ever loved anyone. Lord, please help me get to the bottom of all of this stuff. But mostly, Lord, may your will be done. I have obviously already messed things up enough. Your way, your plan, always." Collin lifted his head, opened his eyes, and looked towards the playground, and there, as plain as day, was his

Delaney going down a toddler slide with a mini version of himself sitting on her lap. Collin froze. Suddenly, Collin knew Jesus was with him. God had been listening.

Chapter 12

The park seemed like a great idea after the huge lunch!

Riley had been healing up nicely, but a couple gentle trips down the slide on his mom's lap and some swinging was more than enough action for the little man's day!

While they gently swung, Delaney decided to share a little more about her and Riley's situation. She told Anna that she came from Tigard, Oregon and had attended Tigard High. She told her about how she had been on the swim team, and how she had loved to sing and play the piano. Delaney also, for the first time, told someone about Collin. Her first love, the man she thought she would spend the rest of her life with, her forever. She told Anna how one night, one time had changed everything. She wouldn't trade Riley for the world, but she sure wished the circumstances were different.

Delaney was starting to get chilly and she and Anna decided to head back to their cars. Delaney wanted to get Riley down for a little nap and clean the house before Jessica came home. It was 3:30 already. Time flies! Anna reached over and gave Delaney a little hug and told her she was there if Delaney needed to talk. And they set up a time to meet again on Wednesday morning! Delaney could not help but think that this was the beginning of a beautiful friendship.

Collin sat frozen in his shadow under the tree. He heard God's voice like He was right beside him: "Be still." Collin sat for a few minutes, first staring at Delaney's soft features, her long, curled blonde hair. He closed his eyes and he could smell her favorite body spray. It was the purple one, from Victoria's Secret. Love something-or-other, it was called. He remembered being too embarrassed to go in the store and asking his mom to purchase it for him at Christmas time just two years ago. It had been her favorite for years. Then he switched his borderline stalker gaze to the adorable little boy on her lap. Delaney was obviously a good mom. She looked so in love with the boy, *his* boy. Collin started to get up. He needed to approach her, even in his fear. As he began to rise, he heard it again, that still small voice: "Wait."

Collin stopped. *But Lord*, he thought. Finally, he watched Delaney and the little guy stand up. She was with another woman who looked older than Delaney. A friend of hers maybe, or a relative? Collin was not aware of Delaney having an aunt or cousin in Washington, but you never know! The two women started to walk away. Collin wanted to run to them, but somehow he knew it was wrong. So he stayed put, not out of cowardice, but out of obedience. Collin began to pray. This time, he prayed that God would show him a plan for redemption. It was something only God could do! No more fear. It was time to be brave.

John James loved being with his boys. He also loved dirt bikes, so any day spent with both was a good day. The boys had ridden for about an hour when they decided to pull off and pulled out the lunches Anna packed for them. John made small talk with the boys for a few minutes. They chatted about school, church, and home life. John got Ben talking about wrestling, and before they knew it, Blake and John were both laughing hysterically as Ben told funny stories about his team.

"So, you really like wrestling?" John asked as they finished up the last bites of their sandwiches.

"I really do, Dad," Ben said. "Lately I just find myself being frustrated about a lot of things. When I wrestle, I get to let out some of that frustration."

"What are you frustrated about?" John asked his son, hoping he would feel safe enough to open up out here in the middle of nowhere.

"I don't know. I guess sometimes I feel like no one gets me, ya know? I feel like I make way more mistakes than I should. I get angry, sometimes with other people, sometimes with myself for not being able to handle it. I just get so frustrated with everything."

"You know what, son? I had so many times of feeling like that growing up." John paused for a moment and looked Ben in the eyes. "It is hard being a kid in the spotlight and feeling like the world always expects you to do the right thing. You just need to remember: no one is perfect, and your mom and I don't expect you to be."

"Are you sure about that, Dad?" Ben scowled as he spoke, "because sometimes Mom is really hard on me."

"I am sure she is, Ben," John said with a smile. "Your mom has been under a lot of stress lately with the play coming up fast, among other things. I don't think she means to be hard on you. Your mom just sees your potential and wants to see you succeed and do great things. We are both so proud of the young men you two are becoming. If we ever seem hard on you, it is because we know how huge your talents and potential are. We only push you to help you be the best you can be!" John was earnest as he went on. "I love you boys so much. I am the luckiest guy alive. I have a wife who loves me and three kids who totally rock. Now," John said, "enough with the mushy stuff. Let's ride before we run out of time."

Chapter 13

The next two weeks were a blur. Anna had had coffee twice now with Delaney, and the young woman was really beginning to open up. They were sharing devotions together, and Delaney was starting to see God as more than rules and judgment. Delaney even came to dinner once at the James' house. The kids just loved her. They also loved Riley! What a sweet little boy. Blake and Ben took turns playing with him. Ben had a real knack for making little Riley laugh. And Blake blew bubbles with him, which Riley though was hilarious.

Delaney was really settling in. The play was in two days and tomorrow was dress rehearsal. Delaney offered to help Anna with the details, since she had loved musical theater growing up in Oregon. Delaney was a natural with the kids, and Blake was more than willing to hang out with his new little buddy Riley.

Anna loved watching Blake with kids. He was a child magnet for sure. Anna saw the sweetest, kindest parts of Blake shine through when little people were around. Anna wondered what God was going do with the life of her oldest boy. She could hardly wait to see.

"Okay Brooke, your solo sounds beautiful, but you look like you're sad to be singing it. What's up?" Anna heard Delaney saying to her daughter.

"Ben said I was the Brooklyn Bridge and he was gonna step on me, he hurt my feelings." Anna sat back and smiled as Delaney pepped up Brooke with just the right mix of "boys are dumb" and "buck up and get over it." Anna was impressed.

Tonight had been just a rehearsal for soloists to make sure they were solid before the play. It was definitely time to be done. After the last of the kids was picked up, Delaney asked Anna if it was cool if she sat at the piano for a moment. Of course! Delaney sat down and began to play Anna's favorite hymn. With a smile, Anna stood beside her on the platform.

"You play beautifully."

"Thank you," Delaney said. "My grandmother taught me this song. It was her favorite. She loved it when I played it."

Anna began to sing along to the music Delaney played, and Delaney joined in with a beautiful harmony.

"When peace, like a river, attendeth my way,

When sorrows like sea billows roll;

Whatever my lot, Thou has taught me to say,

It is well, it is well, with my soul."

Blake came up behind her and joined in with a nice tenor; soon Ben was singing too. And in that moment, Anna felt peace—peace both for Delaney and her own current situation. Peace for the day and for the play. Anna whispered a little prayer under her breath for her new friend Delaney, for her kids, and finally for John. Just as she opened her eyes, John walked through the door. It was amazing that after 20 years of marriage, her heart still soared when he walked into a room. Anna suddenly felt a deep sense of well-being. It was all going be just fine, because no matter what happened, God had it all under control. He had never failed her yet.

Franklin Evans wondered to himself if this was some kind of invasion of his daughter's privacy. He had been watching Delaney's card closely lately. He felt a little guilty, and yet, it was still his card. Franklin found some justification in that fact. It was for three weeks now that Delaney's purchases had remained in one general area of

Washington State. She was sticking to a handful of places along or near the Hood Canal, Gig Harbor, Tacoma, Port Orchard, Allyn, and Belfair, but mostly Belfair. Before now, it seemed she never spent more than a few days in any given location. She had lived very frugally, seeming to only purchase necessities, and never anything extravagant. At times he was impressed by her self-control over the last two years. Why had she ended up there? What could Delaney possibly have found in a little town like Belfair?

Franklin hoped there was no boy involved in her sudden decision to stay in one place. He hated to think what could happen if his daughter ever found herself desperate enough. Franklin had done some research on the rural town. Belfair seemed like a quaint little community with wetland walking trails and the beautiful Belfair State Park; however, it also was becoming quite known for its numerous pot shops. Curiosity was getting the better of him. Franklin needed an excuse to go to Washington, and soon lest he go insane with wonder and worry!

Completely unsure about how he was going to do it, Franklin was determined to get himself and his wife to Belfair, Washington for Christmas. His wife Dory had always been a fan of spa resorts. Franklin had spent the prior evening searching for the best spa resorts along the Hood Canal. What he needed was to create a Christmas miracle. And the only miracle Frank wanted was his daughter, safe and sound. Over the last year Dory had become more and more sad and depressed. He hated to see his wife this way, and if Franklin were honest with himself, he knew it had probably been his own sadness and depression that brought his wife to this point.

In Union, Washington, just a few miles from Belfair, Frank found nice resort, and miraculously there was a room available. They would do Christmas this year at the Alderbrook Resort & Spa. Last year, Christmas was miserable. He was starting to think that maybe it wouldn't be that hard to convince Dory to travel for the holiday, to escape all of the family memories that would be amiss this holiday season.

Amazingly, when he brought the idea up to his wife, she readily agreed that maybe a little getaway would do them both some good. With the knowledge that they would be leaving in just two days, Franklin couldn't help but get excited about the prospect. Monday morning they would head out, they would arrive at Alderbrook in Washington by 3:00 p.m.

Franklin had always been somewhat of a religious man; he'd gone to church, although mostly out of a sense of obligation mixed with a little bit of convenience. He had come to find out that going to a church built a name for you in the community, and a good name gave you better sales. But tonight, as Franklin lay in his bed, he began to pray in a different sort of way. Franklin pleaded with God to help him find his little girl.

Chapter 14

As Collin drove home, he began devising a plan of how he was going to get out of Christmas with his parents. The knowledge that Delaney was alive and well in Belfair burned inside him like a raging fire. Tomorrow was Sunday; he could show up at that little Belfair church and create a chance meeting with her. The desire to meet the boy whom he was sure was his own son was making butterflies wreak havoc on his tummy, and giving him an anticipation he could not have imagined.

Collin was falling in love with a baby he had never met. He was wanting, longing even, to hold this little piece of himself. He had so many questions. Were his eyes blue like Delaney's, or brown like his? What color would his hair become? It had seemed from a distance to appear blond, like Delaney's. Where was he born? Was he happy? Was he healthy? Did he smell fresh like baby powder?

Collin had always been the guy who avoided babies. He had never even touched an infant that he could remember. It was not that he didn't like them—he feared them. Those floppy heads and breakable bodies. Had his parents thought that about him? With that thought, Collin pictured his parents. As far back as he could remember, they had always pushed him. In lacrosse it was always *run faster*, and *be aggressive*, and *push harder*. When it came to academics it was *A's, Collin, only A's are acceptable for the Haggerty men.* Even when it came to the friends Collin chose to hang with, only the best kids were suitable for the Haggerty's precious son. Collin always appreciated the fact that his parents wanted the best for him. At times, however, it was seemingly impossible to live under the scrutiny of the senior Haggerty man. Collin thought about the strange feelings he was having toward this little child he had not yet been introduced to. The love he was already feeling was strange. Suddenly, Collin knew he could not skip Christmas with his parents. So what in the world was he going to do?

Wow, what a crazy night! Brooklyn was a bit of a wreck tonight. She seemed to be crying about anything and everything. Anna decided it was time for her to go to bed. How was she going to pull this one off? Anna sauntered over to the clock on the oven and set it ahead by an hour and a half. Brooke did not need to know she was heading to dreamland a bit early tonight.

Anna quietly filled the boys in on the plan and announced to everyone it was bedtime. Had to love the darkness of wintertime; Anna could have never pulled this off in July. Now Brooke was finally asleep and the boys were watching a movie in their room. The dress rehearsal had been nothing short of disastrous. Their live baby Jesus cried through the whole performance, causing several kids to get distracted and forget the words to their solos—Brooklyn included. Two of the angels had chicken pox, and Joseph was suspended from school for bringing fireworks to class. Anna had spent 20 minutes on the phone with the kid's mother, begging her to *please* let him be in the Christmas program, even though the kid was doomed to be grounded for life. Finally, his mother agreed to let him do it, but not until after Anna sweated a bit more than she had planned for the day.

Anna caught the aroma of coffee and walked into the kitchen. There at the kitchen bistro table sat John, holding her favorite china mug filled with steaming, wonderful smelling coffee. Oh, how she loved this man. How had she landed this guy? It was God's doing for sure!

"You know what they say: if the dress rehearsal is bad, the play is bound to be great!" John spoke up as Anna inhaled her coffee.

"Well then, this play is gonna be fabulous."

"I cannot believe you got Ricky's parents to agree to let him play Joseph tomorrow. I heard they were steaming at the ears after school on Friday."

"Well," Anna said, "I guess I have the magic touch!"

"They didn't want to let you down!"

"Well I am glad, because I don't want to let everyone else down."

"It is going to be great. You have worked so hard on this production. Everyone will come through. Just let God handle the worrying. Okay? Because I want to snuggle on the couch with my wife, watch a little TV, and then go snuggle some more." John chuckled at Anna, sipping her coffee. "It amazes me how you can drink coffee at 7:30 p.m. and still be dead to the world by 10:30. I would be awake all night."

"It is a gift, I guess," Anna said, walking into John's arms and snuggling into that place at his chest that seemed made just for the shape of her. "This is exactly what I need for tonight. How did I get so blessed as to have you to keep me sane?" She asked.

"I know. I am pretty terrific, aren't I?" As John and Anna sat together watching episodes of Blue

Bloods on Netflix, they both had the feeling they didn't want be anywhere else.

Collin's friends all left the previous week for the holiday, and Collin went home to spend a couple days with his folks. But now, here he was, back in Belfair. He found himself sitting in the O'Reilly's parking lot on the eve of Christmas Eve. He was determined to work up the nerve to head into that church this morning. *Lord, help me please. I know this is what I need to do, but I am so scared. What if she is done with me? What if she blames me for ruining her life?* Collin decided to entertain no more destructive thoughts. In those horrible weeks after he had feebly tried to end his life, his friend Jax had told him how important it was for him to think positively. He opened his car door and headed to the cross walk between the auto parts store and the church across the street.

When Collin walked into the church, he was greeted by children in angel costumes handing out programs for the service that morning. They were so adorable, with their glittered hair and tinsel wings. It took him only a minute to realize that this church had a balcony, and Collin began to make his way up the stairs. He chose a seat where he could see the most of the happenings below. That is when he saw her.

Delaney was sitting in the second row near the front of the stage, talking to a lady old enough to be her mother. The two women seemed to be very familiar with each other. Collin sat and watched the interaction between Delaney and the lady with the beautiful long brown hair. Delaney seemed so comfortable here. She looked so peaceful. For a moment, Collin thought about moving down and sitting on the ground level closer to her. Just then, the lights dimmed and the sweetest little girl began to sing a song about Jesus being the best gift of all this Christmas. Collin wondered if Delaney had found that gift, like he had a year and a half ago when the love of his life ran away with his heart. Had she found Jesus in this tiny town?

Anna was so proud of Brooke. She remembered every word of her solo that started off the kids' program. She sang like an angel and the congregation erupted in applause when she finished. Anne watched Delaney as Brooke sang and saw a look of pride on the young woman's face, knowing she had worked with Brooke this week perfecting the phrases as they sang together. Delaney and Brook had really connected.

All the angels spoke their lines perfectly, and each shepherd sang his song with vigor. Joseph showed up and Mary held baby Jesus in calm, tantrum-less sleep. Anna was so pleased. *Thank you, Lord!* As the play finished and the children filed off to the kids church room, Delaney got up and followed. She headed to the student center to help get the kids out of their costumes and out to their parents in the lobby, where they would all enjoy coffee, cocoa, and cookies. While an ensemble of carolers Anna had pulled together sang in the corner of the foyer, Anna paused and wondered how she had ever managed before Delaney had come along. Then she made her way to the student center to help hurry the kids along.

Collin noticed that Delaney got up and left with the kids and he found himself descending the balcony stairs while the congregation was still holding their candles in the sanctuary, singing "Silent Night". Delaney had not been holding a baby this time, and as Collin walked down the stairs, he saw signs that pointed to the nursery. Could his child be hanging out in the nursery with the other little people? He stopped along the wall of the nursery room that had tinted, one-direction windows. There, sitting in a little chair close to the ground, sat the cutest blond-haired, blue-eyed boy he had ever seen. The child had Delaney's button nose and elfish ears, and Collin stared into little eyes that looked just like his own. Collin suddenly felt like it was not the right time to be here in this place, and he turned to walk away.

At that moment, he saw a man looking at him curiously. The man came over to him, held out his hand, and said, "Hi, I am John James. Welcome to our church and Merry Christmas." Collin took John's hand and said hello in return. Collin told the very nice man that he was just visiting from Northwest University. John shared that he and his wife had met at NU, and they had a nice little conversation about how much the school has changed over the years. John asked Collin what his Christmas plans were, and Collin shared that he didn't really have any. Collin realized how strange that would sound to this guy, since it was just two days before Christmas. John told Collin that the church had a Christmas Eve service the next day, and that Collin was welcome to come spend Christmas with the James family if he needed a place to have a nice dinner.

John explained that there would be another young lady spending Christmas at his family's house as well "I am sure she is about your age," he said, "the more the merrier!" Collin suddenly thought, what was the chance that it was Delaney who was going to be at the James' home for Christmas? Collin found himself accepting the invite without another thought. This could end up being one interesting Christmas. Collin readied himself to leave after acquiring directions to John and Anna's house, then hurried to his car. He had booked a room at a hotel in Port Orchard for the night and was ready to get some McDonalds and get checked in. He needed to sit and ponder about what in the world God had in store for him this Christmas. He had a kid and he had found Delaney! Suddenly, everything was coming together in his mind. As much as he was in shock, he was also terrified, yet as much as he was terrified, he was also full of anticipation to talk to the lost love of his life, and to meet his handsome baby boy.

Chapter 15

Franklin and Dolores Haggerty drove down Highway 3 on their way to the Alderbrook Resort & Spa. This really was some picturesque area. As they took the exit toward Union on Highway 106, the drive along the water became simply beautiful. Frank watched all the lovely, quaint little homes along the water as they drove. Suddenly, he did a double take. He was sure he saw Delaney's Jeep parked in one of the driveways along the road across from the water! The letters *QHT* on the Oregon license plate was all he needed to see to know that he was not losing his mind. Yes, that was indeed the car he had gotten his baby girl for graduation just over two years ago.

Frank looked over at Dory, who had closed her eyes to rest. Under his breath, Frank did something he had not done in a very long time. He prayed.

"Dear God, I know she is here. I don't know why, but please help us to find her and please help her to be happy to see us. If she didn't want to see me, I am sure my heart would break. Protect her, Jesus, and protect Dolores' heart. I don't think she could handle it if she lost Delaney again! Amen." Frank suddenly knew he had to find his baby girl, if it was the last thing he did.

The Christmas Eve service came and went in a blur. Anna really enjoyed her family all sitting together in the pew. The years seemed to be flying by, and she wondered just how many more she would have with everyone together. After the service ended, John drove the family to June and Calvin's house for some more family fun. On the way to their house, Anna was thinking about how blessed she was to have such wonderful in-laws when John spoke up.

"I was really hoping to see a new kid tonight that I had invited to service on Sunday. Collin, I think his name was. He seemed like a real nice kid. He didn't have anywhere to be for Christmas."

"Oh, bummer he didn't show!" Anna replied.

"Yeah, he was a student at NU this last year and was just passing through and checking out the church."

"Hmm. That is interesting," Anna replied. "Delaney is coming for dinner tomorrow, right?"

"Yep, I think she is. I was thinking that this Collin guy might enjoy hanging out with a sweet, pretty girl like her."

"Wow, matchmaking is usually my department," Anna said with a laugh.

"No, it is not quite like that." John smiled. "He just seemed sad somehow, kind of like Delaney does sometimes. Although Delaney does seem a lot better since she has been hanging out with you," he said thoughtfully.

"Well, she recommitted her life to Jesus last week when we were out to coffee," Anna said. "I think it is Jesus and not me who is making the difference in her joy level."

John reached over and took Anna's hand. "I am glad Jesus could use you to make a difference in her life," he told her. "She really is a sweet girl." As they pulled into the elder James family's driveway, Anna had one last thought and she spoke it out loud.

"I think Delaney's ex-boyfriend's name was Collin. That might be a little awkward for poor Delaney. Maybe it was for the best."

"Well, I also invited him for dinner tomorrow. I doubt he will show, though, since he didn't show up for tonight's service."

"John, you amaze me. That was very nice of you to reach out to that boy. I guess we will see. It's all in the Lord's hands now."

Collin decided not to show up again at the Belfair church. He was very unsure about what he would do if Delaney saw him there. He had no idea what he would say. How would he explain why he was there? But the more he prayed about it, the more he was sure he needed to show up at John and Anna James' house for Christmas dinner. It seemed like the perfect chance to spend time with some great Christian people.

There was something about John James. He had seemed so real, so genuine. He didn't put on airs or need to be more than who he was. He was simply approachable. Collin had not felt at all intimidated by the man as they talked. Quite the contrary, John seemed like a guy whom Collin could really enjoy hanging out with, even if he was a little old. Who knew? This could also be Collin's chance to be in the same place as Delaney. What in the world was he doing? *Oh God,* he thought, *please help me to do the right thing. Please help me to get the chance to see her. And even if it is time for Delaney and I to be apart, please at least let me have the chance to see her again and to meet my child.*

Collin didn't know if he was going to be able to sleep tonight. But tomorrow was Christmas, and he would pray for a Christmas miracle. Heaven knew he needed one.

Anna and John walked in the door of their house on Christmas Eve at about 10:15 p.m. After finally scooting everyone into bed, the two of them dug out the stocking stuffers and the doll house that still needed to be constructed, and set to work. As tired as she was, Anna loved this part of Christmas. As she gently fingered the special things she put in each stocking, Anna remembered how much she had loved stockings as a child. Stockings had been a tradition her mother kept up, even in the toughest of times after Anna's parents divorced. Anna knew her mother scrimped and saved to be able to put those little treasures into her Christmas stocking. And Anna loved to see the joy on her own children's faces when they opened their own stockings on Christmas morning.

Anna had entered a new place in life. Being a mom was no longer about wiping noses and changing diapers, but about listening to dreams and encouraging futures in her kids. Anna had reached the part of life where she could see each day passing by, and it was all happening too fast. She would cherish this Christmas, and take it moment by moment instead of day by day! She didn't want to miss even a second of the time she had left with the precious kids God had entrusted to her and John's hands.

As John added the finishing touches to the dollhouse that Brooklyn was going to love, Anna set to work in the kitchen, setting the morning cinnamon rolls into the pan to rise. In about six hours, the kids would wake to see what their stockings held for them this year, and she and John would lovingly watch their elated surprise.

Anna had one final task before bed. She needed a little something for this Collin boy, should he show up for Christmas. She dug in the bin in her closet and pulled out a pair of men's driving gloves and a travel coffee mug from the package she had bought in bulk at Costco. Anna always tried to keep some stuff in her bin for any occasion. You never knew when you would need a birthday gift, or a Christmas gift, as today would have it.

Anna felt John walk up behind her. "Well, the dollhouse is assembled! What a pain. But man, Brooky is going to love it."

"She sure will," Anna said as she turned around, resting her head on John's strong chest. "Thanks for doing that!"

"Of course," John said as he softly kissed the top of her head. "Are you ready to hit the hay? The kids will be up in six hours."

"Yep, let me just stick these into a bag."

"Let me guess—just in case Collin shows up?"

"Yes," Anna said with a snicker.

John smiled. "You never cease to amaze me, you know?"

"I know I am crazy, but you are stuck with me," she teased playfully.

"And I wouldn't have it any other way."

Anna hugged him. "I love you, John James. Merry Christmas!"

Chapter 16

Collin dug through his suitcase trying to decide what to wear. He had really filled out a lot since he last saw Delaney. Even after having a baby she still looked flawless, a beautiful picture of perfection. Collin knew he was more muscled now for sure, but as he stood in the mirror, he couldn't help but wonder if Delaney would still be attracted to him.

There had been a time when they both desired nothing more than to be in each other's arms. Would she still want him? Or would she see him as the source of the pain and loss she had most likely experienced throughout the last year and a half? Collin began to wonder if showing up at the James' door was the right thing to do. He guessed that he was about to find out.

He finally pulled out the blue sweater his mother bought him before he went to Northwest University. His mom had said it brought out the color of his eyes. She had assured him of that, just as she assured him there were so many more fish in the sea and that he needed to get over the loss of his first love. Collin had fought those words, and his heart had won.

"Okay, trusty sweater, do your thing," he muttered to himself. "Make me irresistible."

With one last prayer for wisdom, Collin Haggerty walked out the door of his room at the Port Orchard Days Inn, into his uncertain future in Belfair, Washington.

"Are you sure you don't want to come along?" Delaney asked Jessica. "Anna said you were welcome to join us at their house."

"No, honey, I may stop by June and Calvin's house this afternoon for leftovers, but I think I am going to spend this morning curled up with some old home videos. I don't think I am quite ready to be around the family Christmas morning thing yet."

Delaney totally understood. Over the last couple of weeks, Jessica had begun sharing pieces of her tragic story. Jessica had suffered many losses. Less than two years ago, she lost her daughter and her husband on the same day in a tragic accident. Jessica's daughter Chloe was only fifteen years old. To Delaney, is sounded like Chloe Winters had everything going for her. She was beautiful, had a 4.0 GPA, and wanted to be like her mother and had already chosen to attend the University of Washington—Jessica's alma mater. Jessica's husband Rick and Chloe were hit head on by a drunk driver one day on their way home. No one survived.

Jessica was unsure about things this Christmas. Last year, she took extra hours at the hospital doing rounds and even helping in the ER during the Christmas season. This year, however, with Delaney and Riley, things seemed a little more manageable. Jessica still knew so little about Delaney. She had concluded that the girl grew up in Oregon. Jessica also believed that there was a family out there somewhere, enduring a lot of unnecessary pain surrounding the circumstances of Riley's birth. What Jessica couldn't quite put her finger on, was if Delaney's parents even knew the baby existed. All in due time.

Jessica prayed often for this young lady living under her roof. Delaney reminded her so much of Chloe. Beautiful, so much going for her . . . then stunted by life circumstances. There was no hope for Chloe. She was gone. Delaney, however, might just be learning how to live again. Jessica Winters would be right by her side, helping her however she could. Delaney was a gift to Jessica, and definitely her Christmas miracle!

As for the matter of going to Anna and John's, Jessica knew that Chloe had been close to Blake James. They were best friends for years. The prospect of hanging out with the James family for Christmas seemed both comforting and heartbreaking at the same time. This day, Jessica would put off the misery for a few more hours and wallow in her pain, drinking coffee, reminiscing, watching old family videos, and crying alone.

Chapter 17

Franklin handwrote the note in his wife's Christmas package. He had purchased a pretty little Pandora charm to go on her bracelet. He had even secretly packed the bracelet in his suitcase so she could wear it on the trip in the next several days to come. The charm he chose was a white primrose meadow charm from the Pandora Rose Collection he knew Dolores loved. Although it would not be the most expensive charm on her wrist, he knew the rose gold made her think of her own mother who had passed away recently.

Back when he was looking at the charms, the little primrose had called out to him, and Franklin thought of how his wife needed renewed life. She had been so sad. She seemed so lost. The delicate pink charm with its white flower spoke to Franklin, right there in the store. It seemed to whisper the essence of new life. Franklin had purchased it without a second thought. Then, that afternoon in his office, he began to compose the words to his wife that were long overdue. Words that needed to be said or else he would lose her for sure.

This last year had already turned her into a shell of who she used to be, but Franklin was beginning to have hope that he was going to give his wife her own Christmas miracle. While she was basking in a day of pampering at the Alderbrook on Christmas, Franklin would set out on a hunt for the perfect gift, their precious little girl.

Getting ready to walk out the door with Riley in her arms, Delaney heard Jess call her name from the other room.

"Wait, I never gave you your Christmas gift!" Jessica called.

"Are you kidding me?" Delaney said in shock as she closed the door and walked back into the entry way. "You do not need to give me anything. I am so thankful for you! I don't know where I would be without you. Not to mention all you have done for Riley. You saved both of our lives!"

"I am so glad to help, sweetheart, but still I have a gift for you!" Delaney sat little Riley down on the fluffy bear rug on the floor and took the beautiful box from Jessica's hands. Sitting on the sofa, Delaney unwrapped the bow from the perfectly wrapped parcel.

"I hate to unwrap it, it is so perfect!" She murmured. Jessica smiled down at her as she untied the ribbon. Inside the box was a beautiful leather bound Bible. Delaney was suddenly overwhelmed and the tears fell quickly down her cheeks. "Oh, Jessica, it is beautiful!" Delaney took the book out of the box and fingered the pages. They were so thin, yet felt somehow full of strength in her hands. "I don't know what to say—this is so thoughtful of you."

"Just say you will read it. Just say you will consider giving Jesus a chance."

"Oh Jessica, I will and I have! I have decided it is time to commit my life to the Lord for real this time! If I have discovered anything since Riley's surgery and coming to live with you, it is that there is definitely a God out there, and He doesn't hate me." Delaney wiped a tear from her face. "In fact, quite the contrary—He is looking out for me and my son. I think I owe Him my life at this point. And that day at the hospital, the day it all came together and Riley pulled through, I made a promise to God that I would give Him a chance. And . . . well . . . I have seen miracle after miracle since that day.

"It is kind of like that song, "It Is Well," that my grandma used to play. For the first time in forever, I have peace. Even though I know the storm is far from over, I have peace that there is hope for my future. Hope even for me and my parents. Who knows? Maybe there is even hope for me and Collin." Delaney suddenly stood up. "Hey, I almost forgot! I have something for you too! It isn't much, but I made it for you."

Delaney ran up the stairs to her room and then quickly ran back down. In her hand, with no wrapping save a simple red bow, Delaney held a picture frame. She hugged the front of the frame close to her, not letting Jessica see what it held.

"Jessica," she said timidly, "I am a little nervous about this. Please don't be angry with me! I am sorry if it is upsetting. But Anna James helped me find this. Actually, Blake had it in his room."

Jessica felt a knot forming in the pit of her stomach. As she took the frame from Delaney's hand she saw the most beautiful picture of her whole family—Chloe, Rick, and herself. Jessica remembered that day the Winters and the James families had decided to go hiking. It was only a month or so before the accident, a spring break hike up the trails around Lake Cushman. Chloe had taken a picture of Blake's family, and Blake had taken a picture of the Winters. Now it was Jessica's turn to cry!

"Thank you, Delaney Evans! You are a Godsend."

Now running late to get to the James' house for cinnamon rolls and coffee that were promised to be heavenly, Delaney hugged Jessica one last time and headed out the door. Jessica knew she was going to be okay, because God had sent her two angels this Christmas in the form of Delaney and Riley Evans.

Chapter 18

Delaney sat in her Jeep, just as the first of many silver dollar-sized snowflakes began to fall from the sky. More than once, Delaney had heard Ben James express his strong desire for a white Christmas. He was going to be thrilled. Delaney was happy to be getting on the road before the flakes began to stick. By the time she and Riley passed the church, the roads were starting to glisten with white. Delaney had planned to stop at Safeway to pick up a poinsettia for Anna, but decided against it as the space in front of her car whitened.

The hill up to the James' house was steep. Delaney prayed her car would make it. It was not in her plans for the morning to carry Riley up a monster hill in the freezing snow. She sighed in relief when she pulled into the half-moon driveway of the modest house. The trees had turned white here in the higher elevation. It was beautiful. Delaney had risen early this morning and gotten Riley ready in his red Christmas hat and sweater, crocheted by her new friend Lilly. He looked like a toasty little elf. Lilly had promised to teach Delaney the basics of crocheting after New Year's.

Delaney bundled Riley in one arm, gathered some Christmas packages in the other, and awkwardly headed up the stairs to the door, leaving footprints in the freshly fallen snow. She was hoping she had not missed too much of the morning festivities.

"I'm getting up!" Blake James said as his mother came into his room singing a melodious "rise and shine". Ben was already up and waiting in his room, and Brooklyn was in the process of pulling herself out of bed as well. Since when did the mom have to get the kids out of bed on Christmas morning? Delaney would be here in minutes, and the smell of freshly baked cinnamon rolls was already filling the house! Blake groaned and started to pull the covers back over his face.

"Whoa, I think not!" Anna poked his sides and Blake gave a small laugh accompanied by a reluctant, "Fine!" The kids filed out of their rooms, ready to open their stockings. There was a knock at the door just as Blake and Ben rounded the corner in their flannel pajamas. Delaney came in with packages for each family member in her arms. The young woman turned to the kids just in time to see the look of shock and stunned amazement in Brooklyn's eyes as she saw her giant Costco-sized dollhouse that filled the living room. Tears once again filled Delaney's eyes as she saw the excitement unfold.

This was going to be one of those days. Last year at this time, Delaney was eight months pregnant and spent the holiday at the Westfield Mall movie theater. She watched four movies that day, one right after the other. Delaney was still running scared at that time and had purchased gift cards for the AMC Theater a Wal-Mart in Marysville, Washington, just in case her dad was tracking her expenses and following where her card was used.

She didn't allow frivolous expenditures like that, but she had told herself it was Christmas so it was okay to indulge for once. She had been so cold, and it was so wonderful to relax in the soft reclining seats and get lost in the life of someone else for a change. She slept through most of the last movie and was woken up by the theater attendant. He was all flirtatious smiles until she stood up and he saw her protruding stomach. Then he was quick to say *have a nice day* and headed back up the dimly lit aisle way. Delaney had been thankful for the little guy growing inside of her, as he kept the stupid, hormone-raging boys away. Delaney had eyes only for Collin, and he was a world away.

Pulling herself back to the present, Delaney watched the James kids open their stockings. Then they all ate the cinnamon rolls Delaney had been drooling over since she caught her first whiff as she walked through the door.

Blake and Ben began passing out the other gifts and they all sat in the living room, still in their pajamas. Anna's gift sat unopened on the floor in front of her as she watched everyone else open theirs. This was her favorite part. She loved to see these people smile.

Blake opened his box set of Star Wars movies with big eyes. "Dude you got them all!" He exclaimed as he intently studied the back of each set.

Ben was gleaming from ear to ear as he unwrapped the Millennial Falcon in Lego pieces. "I can't wait to put this together! Are you gonna do it with me, Dad?" Ben asked John.

"Of course I am, bud!" Ben beamed with excitement. Anna knew he would enjoy the time spent with his father as much as he would enjoy assembling the craft, if not more.

John opened the box in from of him that held a beautiful watch. Anna had given up her Starbucks coffee for over a month in order to save for it. She was thrilled to see that John seemed to love it. Brooklyn opened up little dolls and furniture that had come with her house, and the boys each had a pocket knife John had picked out especially for them. Anna's heart was full! As she breathed in the aroma of her coffee, she wondered if life could get any better than this.

Her thoughts were interrupted by Delaney asking Ben if he had had a chance to peek outside yet. Ben started doing some kind of crazy dance as he realized his dream of a white Christmas came true! They opened all the blinds and watched the snow fall.

Brooklyn came to Anna and asked, "Mommy, aren't you gonna open your gifts? What about you, Delaney? Oh, and Riley has some too." Delaney looked overwhelmed and Anna wished she could make it all better, but Delaney appeared to be learning what it felt like to have people care about you. Anna knew that feeling could be overpowering.

Delaney picked up a box from the ground in front of her and handed it to little Riley to open. He was not very impressed with the clothes inside, but seemed perfectly happy with the box and the paper it had been wrapped in. Anna watched as Delaney picked up the box with her own name on it. She opened it to find matching PJs, just like the ones the James family was wearing.

"Pajamas are a tradition around here for the James family, and we want you to know we think of you like family!" Anna explained. Delaney beamed.

"Thank you so much!" She squealed. Next, she opened a box with a hat, gloves, and a scarf in it. And finally, she opened a small bracelet that was strung with small, pink ceramic beads that had white flowers on them.

"Those are primroses," Anna told her. "Brooklyn picked it out for you."

"I thought they were so pretty. Just like you, Delaney!" Brooke told her.

"Thank you, Brooke, I love it."

"Mom," Blake said, "you are the only one left. Open your gifts!"

"Okay," Anna answered with a smile. First, she opened a beautiful coffee mug from Ben painted with little blue flowers, and then a box of K-cups from Blake. "You guys know me too well," she told them. Blake and Ben shared a high five.

"We are pretty good," Blake said. Next, Anna opened a pair of cute heart earrings from Brooke with a necklace that said *Mom*, surrounded by a rhinestone heart.

"Because you're the best mom ever!" Brooke said, falling into her mom's lap with a laugh. "And I paid for it all by myself."

"You are the sweetest." Brooklyn ate up the praise from her mom.

"One more," John said, handing Anna a small box. Anna shook it a bit, but the box sounded empty. Curious, she opened the lid to find a piece of folded paper crammed snugly inside. Anna took it out and unfolded it. It was a reservation for the beach, Best Western, for tomorrow!

"No way!" Anna screamed. "You're kidding me, John. I thought you had to work all through the weekend? What happened to 'I am not gonna be able to get any time off this year'?"

"I lied" he stated with a smile.

"John James, I love you! I prayed for a getaway!"

"I love you too!"

"And guess what, Mom?" Interjected Ben. "We are already packed! Dad made us do it so you wouldn't have to."

"Okay, I love you even more now, Mr. James. You are my favorite!" John reached down and gave Anna a kiss.

"Get a room, you guys," Blake said with an over exaggerated grimace, "that is gross."

"Whatever," John said, giving his wife one last kiss. "She likes me."

"Whatever!" Blake said.

"Can we go out into the snow?" Ben asked.

"Wait one second," Delaney said, "I have a little something for all of you." Brooke opened up some fuzzy socks with panda heads on them.

"They're so cute! I love pandas!" Brook squealed.

"I know you do," Delaney said. The boys each opened big boxes of their favorite candies.

"She loves us," Ben said. Delaney laughed, and Blake rolled his eyes at his brother.

"Thanks Delaney, that was cool of you to get us gifts," Blake said.

"You are welcome!" She answered back, "I just wish it could have been more." Ben assured her that it was the thought that counts, receiving yet another eye roll from his brother.

"Yeah, what Ben said," Blake added, causing them all to laugh again. Delaney got John a beef summer sausage, not sure what to get for a man who was worlds different than her father. For Anna, she had purchased a floating key chain.

"Let me guess—this is so I don't lose my keys the next time I go kayaking."

"Yep," Delaney said with a smile. Anna then told everyone the story of how she had dropped and nearly lost her car key the last time she was out on the Canal with Jessica. She ended up having to actually get into the water. After a ten minute search that felt like an hour, she had miraculously found the key again.

"We just about froze to death," she told them. The boys were laughing, but John looked serious.

"And why did you not tell me this story before today?" He demanded. "You could have gotten hypothermia!"

"But I didn't," Anna said.

"Okay, fine." He retreated. "You amaze me, my dear," he said under his breath.

"And he wonders why I kept quiet," Anna joked to Delaney. "Well, this was all very thoughtful of you," she continued.

"I know it is not much you guys, but I am very thankful for all of your kindness. Money is a little tight," said Delaney.

"It's okay," answered Brook, "after all, you know it's the thought that counts." She was repeating her brothers' words and they all smiled at Brooke and her sweetness.

"Oh, sure, it's cute when she says it," complained Ben.

"Shut up, Ben," Blake said.

"Enough, both of you," John finished. "I hear the snow calling."

"Snow ball fight!" The James boys yelled in unison.

"Okay," Anna said, "let's clean up this mess and then you have about two hours to play in the snow before we head to Grandma and Grandpa's house."

"Okay!" They all said, and got to work tidying up the front room and dressing in their warm clothes for the snow war that was about to take place. Then they would do a little sledding while the snow was fresh. It had really started to accumulate and was still coming down like crazy.

"I love the snow, thank you Jesus!" Ben shouted as he slammed the door and headed for the snowy hill.

"I wanted to let you know, there is a slim chance we could have one more visitor today for Christmas dinner," John told Delaney. The three of them now sat drinking coffee while the kids continued to play outside in the snow. "This young man came to church last week and I felt compelled to invite him today. He seemed so lost and had nowhere to be for Christmas."

"No worries here," Delaney said, "I have this awesome man repellant called a baby." She finished with a grin, "I rarely have to worry about boys."

"His name is Collin," Anna said with her eyebrows raised. "I thought you might want to be preparing for that one."

"Wow, thanks Anna," said Delaney appreciatively.

"He is a first year student at Northwest University in Kirkland. He is studying to be a pastor. Yet, there was something about this kid that made me feel like he could benefit from some time spent hanging out with a pastor's family. He just seems sad, I guess. I think that he is about your age, Delaney. He didn't seem like someone looking for a relationship. More like someone looking for a friend."

"Well, we can all use a friend," Delaney said.

"That's what I thought. It is a pretty slim chance he will actually show up, but I gave him directions to my parents' house. And he said he might, so we will see."

With that, John decided that with the way the snow was falling, they should head to his folks' house sooner than later. The kids weren't too disappointed because the elder James' house had an even cooler sledding hill.

Collin was ready to go. The thought of spending the day with Delaney both excited and terrified him. What if she was not as excited to see him as he was to see her? This could be a disaster for the James' family Christmas. Yet, Collin could not give up on the chance. In his heart, he knew he could not go one more day without trying to make things right. He needed to at least apologize for putting Delaney into this position. He loved her; he wanted to marry her. There was no other girl out there for him, and he would spend the rest of his life trying to show her that. Delaney was everything that was good in his life. She *got* him. She understood his overbearing parents. She understood his stuffy "follow in your father's footsteps" kind of life. And she had loved him anyway, despite all of his crazy life. Delaney Evans had been in love with him. A little snow on the roads was not going to deter him from seeing her today. As a matter of fact, the snow might just make this day that much more magical.

Collin put his winter boots on his feet, slipped on his coat, and pulled out of the hotel driveway at 12:15. His GPS said he would arrive in Grapeview, Washington at 12:57. With the snow on the roads, who knew? But dinner was at 2:00 and John had said he could show up any time after 1:00. He simply couldn't wait another moment. Collin suddenly felt desperate. He had to see her in person.

Chapter 19

Dory and Franklin had a lovely Christmas brunch at the resort restaurant. Now they were on their way back to their room to exchange gifts. Dory was more than a little bit curious to see what was hidden in the beautiful little box under the miniature tree in their room. She had thought long and hard about what to get Franklin for Christmas this year. Dolores felt so disconnected from him since Delaney ran away. She had tried so hard to not be angry at Franklin for not searching harder to find their daughter. Over the years, Dolores had become so dependent on Frank for everything. But soon, all that was going to end. If Franklin really cared, he would be looking for his daughter. Dolores loved her husband, but she knew it was time for a change. She would enjoy this last trip with Franklin Evans and then, when they returned home next week, she would give the man she loved an ultimatum.

He would either hire private investigators to find their daughter, or she would herself. And if he said no, Dolores was going to leave him. She could no longer go on this way, living as a shell of the woman she once was. Depression had dug its talons in her so deeply that she didn't know how to get free. From the death of her mother to the moment

Delaney ran away from home, Dolores felt more and more hopeless. She had no control. And now, she was only a few small steps away from tossing away the one good thing she had left in her life.

Her light had simply gone out. Whether he realized it or not, letting Frank go was what was best for him. She was the anchor tied around his ankle that would eventually drag him to his emotional death as well. The only light she saw at the end of this dark tunnel was locating her only child. Dolores needed to find Delaney. If she couldn't, Dolores did not know if she could carry on. She knew she definitely couldn't continue the way things were now.

As the two of them walked back through the halls to their room, Dolores found herself whispering a prayer to the Lord, that her husband of 23 years would want to find their daughter. Because suddenly, Dolores didn't know what she would do if she had to lose him, too.

Collin was surprised to see as he drove through town that the Belfair Safeway was open. And as much as he hated the thought of supporting the fact that the store was open on Christmas morning, he also hated the thought of showing up empty handed at the James' house. He quickly trudged into the store, grabbing a chocolate Santa and a movie gift card for each of the James kids; a poinsettia for Mrs. James and her mother-in-law; and a beef summer sausage gift box for both John and his dad. Collin also piled a handful of other Christmas candies into his cart for whoever else might be at the dinner today. Now, he just needed something for the baby. The baby with Delaney's hair and his eyes. He found a cute stuffed monkey with a Santa hat for the little guy, and then grabbed a Babies 'R' Us gift card. The card could be loaded with $15-$500. Collin was so nervous that he had no idea how much to make it good for. But since he had missed everything in that child's life up to now, $500 seemed like nothing compared to what he owed the kid.

Collin didn't need to find anything for Delaney; he had already taken care of that when he went home to Tigard earlier that week. He had her small gift tucked into the pocket of his jacket. Every few minutes he found himself tapping his pocket to make sure it was still there. Collin did, however, grab a $100 Starbucks card to use as a back-up, just in case the gift in his pocket seemed out of place for today. Delaney loved coffee. And finally, Collin grabbed a couple bottles of sparkling cider as a final touch, and headed to the checkout line to pay.

Collin was beyond nervous as he took the last turn onto the road that led to the James house. But he also held a genuine excitement for what this day could hold. Collin imagined holding his baby boy for the first time. Collin also could not help but imagine his lips on Delaney's. After all this time, he could not fathom that there could be anyone else in the world for him but Delaney Evans. And suddenly, the car could not move fast enough. Collin's stomach was doing flips at the anticipation and excitement. *Oh God, help me. I trust you, Lord. I know you have my back; now if you could just help me not to puke before I get in there . . .*

Chapter 20

Collin could hear the sound of kids playing in the backyard behind the house. As he stepped up to the front door to ring the bell, he was greeted by John, who pulled him into a big hug.

"Wow, I am so glad you decided to come, Collin! The kids are all out playing in the snow. Come on in and have some coffee before it gets crazy in here again."

As soon as he walked in the door, Collin was greeted by three tiny smiles. John introduced Collin to the first two kids as two of his sister's children. He said their names, but Collin could not hear past the drum beating of his heart. He only had eyes for the littlest of the kids at his feet. Reaching down to the floor, Collin picked of the little boy with the beautiful blond curls.

"And who might this be?" Collin asked, trying not to act weird about the possibility that he had just picked up his son for the first time.

"This is Riley Evans. His mom is here somewhere. I think she is in the kitchen helping Grandma June make dinner."

"Riley, huh? That's my name too, little guy— Collin Riley Haggerty. It is very nice to meet you."

"Riley is our little miracle baby," John began to explain. "He almost died this year. He has a rare heart condition called congenital heart disease; this little guy has fought hard to stay alive." John tried to explain how little Riley had an aortic valve that was too small, but that a surgeon from their church had successfully fixed Riley right up! "You're as good as new now, aren't you buddy? He was very lucky to have his momma. She figured out the signs before it was too late and got him medical care just in time. A little emergency lifesaving surgery, and here he is! Good to go, for the most part. We all keep this little man in our prayers and hope for no more complications. We really do serve a mighty God."

Collin just stood there frozen in shock. He had a dumbfounded look on his face. His son had almost died. What had Delaney been forced to go through? And worse, all on her own. Collin was suddenly even more nervous. He wanted to either bolt from the house or curl up on the floor and cry, he wasn't really sure which.

Before he could give it another overwhelming thought, suddenly, from around the corner, came the most beautiful girl he had ever seen. And when she looked up and saw Collin's face, Delaney froze like a deer in headlights, completely stunned. One look at the two kids and John somehow knew that this was *the* Collin. John slipped around the corner, grabbed Anna by the arm, and pulled her into the entryway where Collin and Delaney still looked at each other in stunned silence. Anna gave them one glance and also knew that, by a one in a million chance, this was Delaney's Collin.

"Collin, Delaney, so I take it you have met?" John said matter-of-factly.

"Uhh . . . yeah," Delaney said. Collin still could not find any words to speak. "How . . . how did you find you me? How did you come, did you— what did you . . ." Delaney stumbled over her words as her brain fought to keep up with the new information her eyes were giving her.

"Okay, you two, let's head into the living room," Anna suggested quietly, putting her hand on Delaney's shoulder.

In all their years of ministry, Anna and John James had seen a lot. But this moment surely took the cake.

"Okay, what do we have here?" Anna spoke softly but directly to the two who were both still clearly in shock. "I am gathering, Delaney, that this in *the* Collin Haggerty. From wherever you grew up?"

"Yes," Delaney said quietly. "You are supposed to be in Connecticut—you are supposed to be on the other side of the world, the East Coast? Not the West Coast? Why are you not at Harvard? What are you doing in Belfair? I don't understand." Delaney rambled off question after question. Collin did not want to interrupt her, so he gently reached his hand out and touched her face.

"I can explain," Collin started. "After you disappeared, I was completely lost. You were my everything, Delaney, and without you, I had nothing left! I didn't want to go on anymore without you. Jax noticed my depression and in a last ditch effort to help me, took me to his church. I gave my life to Jesus, for real, and then I decided to go to school for ministry. I am still not exactly sure what I am doing, but now I'm at Northwest University trying to figure it all out. I came to Belfair to ride dirt bikes during the winter break." Collin suddenly wondered how much more he should say. He didn't want to sound like a stalker, as if he had been following Delaney for week, so he treaded a little more carefully.

"Then, not by chance, I ended up at the Belfair church where I met John and he invited me to Christmas dinner. I thought I saw you, but then I saw the baby and I was questioning if it was indeed you and . . . well, I got scared." Collin took a step back and put his head down, ashamed of what a coward he was. John put a hand on his shoulder.

"That must be why you were so unsure about accepting my invitation to Christmas."

"Yes, Mr. James, you are exactly right, and it's also why I didn't make it to the service," Collin said with his head still lowered. Then he nestled into the neck of Riley, who was very cozy and laid back in his father's arms. John broke the momentary silence.

"Well, it was pretty brave of you to show up here today."

"I don't feel so brave here right now, sir. I am actually terrified. But I heard somewhere once that courage is not the absence of fear, but the triumph over it."

"Nelson Mandela," John said.

"Yes sir, that is one of my father's favorite quotes."

"Sounds to me like your dad is a pretty smart guy."

"Yes he is, Mr. James."

"Well," John said, "the fact that you are here right now in my parents' living room says to me that you are one brave, courageous young man."

Delaney finally spoke up. "Okay, so I am confused. You knew I came to Belfair, or at least thought you knew, and you knew that there was a baby, and yet, here you are? Why are you here, Collin?" Collin took a step closer to Delaney, very sure of his next response.

"Because *you* are here, and I love you, Delaney Evans. And life is not the same without you. I have prayed every day since I gave my heart to the Lord, that the Lord would either help me find you, or get you out of my head! I could not forget you; I couldn't get you out of my head, or my heart. "Then finally, on Christmas day a year later, here you are—my Christmas miracle! Delaney, I am so sorry! I am sorry I pressured you into doing things you were not ready for. I am sorry I was not there for you when you were going through what had to be one of the hardest times in your life, and if I am not mistaken, I am sorry that you've felt like you had to raise our son all on your own, and I am sorry I did not work harder to find you."

"Oh Collin, I don't blame you for anything!" Delaney interjected. "I made my choices. And I got pregnant. I was the coward and I ran. I was afraid of what my parents would think, and I was afraid that you would not want me anymore if I ruined your hopes of being what your father wanted you to be. I did not give you the option of choosing Riley and I ran away because I let fear win." Tears were free-falling down Delaney and Collin's faces now. Anna and John were both teary as well.

Delaney continued. "But then, Riley got sick and I learned what real fear is. If I had not met Anna that night in the hospital, and if I had not cried out to God in a last ditch effort to save my baby, and if Dr. Winters had not been there to perform the surgery that saved Riley's life, I don't think I would be around today.

"I made a mistake, Collin—I ran from my problems instead of facing them. But I don't know if I would have decided to give my life completely to the Lord if I had not run. I have no doubt that God brought me to Belfair for a reason. I was lost and He found me. I had no peace in my life. I was like a ship lost at sea, but God sent me a lifeboat when He sent me Anna and Jessica." Delaney reached out and took Collin's hand. "And then, when I was ready, God gave me the one thing I dreamed of having back—my life. And now," she paused to wipe away the tears from her face, "it looks like God brought me you!"

Anna and John got up quietly while Delaney and Collin continued to talk through the last year. Riley seemed to take to Collin like it was meant to be. Anna took a deep breath and walked into John's open arms where he stood. "Wow," she said, "that is God's grace if I have ever seen it."

"Yes, it sure is. I think Collin and Delaney are gonna be just fine."

Chapter 21

Dolores held the box from Franklin in her hands, a little nervous to open it. Franklin had already opened his gift—a new watch that Dolores knew he had been looking at. She had seen it it in his prime account and watched it, knowing it was the perfect gift. It was like a representation of time, something she found herself hoping for. It would be a token that, to Dolores, represented lost time that had to be found. And time spent together, in the future.

Attached to Franklin's gift was a note. She opened it first.

My Dearest Dolores,

This last year and a half has been the hardest time of our married lives. I simply would not have made it through this storm without you. I have been thinking a lot about Delaney lately, and how much we both miss her. I don't know what you think about us trying to find her? I want you to know that if the two of us is all we ever have, I am okay with that. But I want to try to find our little girl. I want to find me again, and I want you to find you again.

Honestly, I think she took pieces of our hearts with her when she left. We are broken and I hate to see you hurting. I say, maybe it is time to see if we can find a new beginning. You have worked so hard holding things together for us, and you deserve a day of pampering. Starting at 3:30 until 6:30 today, the spa is yours. You'll have three hours to unwind and be pampered. Then, when that is over, I want us to make a plan together—how we are going to put our family back together.

This small gift reminded me of life, beautiful and fragile, ready to bloom and grow. I love you, Dolores; I always have and I always will.

Forever yours,

Franklin

Dolores opened the box and held the small Pandora bead in her hand. The rose gold bead was so beautiful. The delicate primroses on it reminded her of her mother and of her daughter, and it was so much more symbolic after reading the words in Frank's note. How, just moments ago, had she been about to give up on this man? Could she have really been ready to let go of the love that they shared? Dolores was convinced that that was what desperation did to you—it crippled you from the inside out and stole away the things that offer any source of hope. But, there was hope! Dolores remembered her simple yet desperate prayer. Hope, there it was. Bold, beautiful, and right there. *Thank you, Jesus,* she rejoiced silently.

Dolores walked over to her husband and put her arms around him for the first time in over a year. "Honey," Dolores said, "I do not want to go to the spa. I want to be with you, and then I want to find our baby girl. I love you and I don't ever want to give up on us, and I don't ever want to give up on our only daughter."

The tears flowed in a steady stream down the face of his wife, and Franklin felt overwhelmed with love for this woman. He wrapped her in an embrace that was long overdue and then kissed her with all the pent up feelings he has inside. As he tasted her tears, he knew they were mingled with his own.

"I am so sorry," he said.

"So am I," Dolores agreed.

Nearly an hour later, snuggled up on the sofa, Franklin told his wife that he believed Delaney was in Belfair. He offered that, if she wanted to take a risk, he might know where she was. Franklin's fear that Dolores would be angry vanished immediately with her look of love and eagerness. The fear was replaced with hope and, fifteen minutes later, Franklin and Dolores Evans were traveling down South Shore Road of the Hood Canal in search of a dream, and Delaney's Jeep Liberty.

Jessica was dozing in her overstuffed chair when she was suddenly awakened by a knock at the door. *Who in the world could be here on Christmas?* She wondered. Jessica had actually meant to be out the door and off to the James' house an hour ago, until she had fallen asleep.

She opened the door and was greeted by a man about her age. He was accompanied by a woman who looked a lot like . . . Delaney?

"Hello," said Jessica, "how can I help you?"

"Well," the small woman said, "We are Frank and Dolores Evans and . . . well . . . we think you may be able to help us. We've lost our daughter, and our search has led us here."

Without another question, Jessica invited the Evans into her home. They chatted about Delaney for about ten minutes, and then Jessica excused herself to make a phone call.

Anna's phone began to ring just as they were standing up from the dinner table. Collin was leading the James kids into the living room to give them the gifts he bought. Anna stepped out onto the front porch to take the call.

"Hello Anna, I am so sorry to bug you, but we need to talk." Jess explained to Anna that Delaney's parents were at her house and that she hoped Anna had some advice on what in the world she was supposed to do with them. Anna, shocked, recounted her own experience from that morning and told Jessica that she had Delaney's long lost love, Riley's father, sitting on her in-laws' living room sofa. Both women needed a moment to regain their composure. The whole scene was nothing short of stunning.

"Anna, I think this may be a Christmas miracle."

"I'm a little afraid I'm going to scare poor Delaney to death if I tell her that her parents are waiting for her at your house."

"I get it completely," Jessica said. "But what am I supposed to do with them in the meantime?"

"I don't know. But I do know this. Collin had no idea he was a father, since as soon as Delaney got close showing her pregnancy she bolted. My guess is that Delaney's parents don't know that they are grandparents. So, I think we should keep that much under wraps. It simply is not our story to tell."

"How did Collin handle things?" Jessica asked Anna.

"He could not have handled it better. He really loves her. Collin Haggerty is going to make a wonderful father. And Riley already seems to be in love. I am so excited for them! Our little girl is gonna be okay! I have a really good feeling about this, Jess."

"Me too," agreed Jessica. "So, we need a plan!"

"I will break the news to Delaney about her parents being in town before she leaves here today. You occupy them until she gets there."

The Evans needed their Christmas miracle too, but Christmas still had several hours left to unfold.

Delaney and Collin told Anna and John that they were going to take a little walk. John explained to Collin how to get down to the beach from his parents' house, and Anna offered to keep Riley, who was just almost asleep, on the couch by Blake and Ben as all of the kids sat watching *How the Grinch Stole Christmas*. Hand in hand, Delaney and Collin walked down to the beach. When they arrived down by the water, Collin wrapped his arms around Delaney's waist.

"I can't believe you are here. I am touching you! You don't hate me! Man, I missed you."

"I missed you too," she spoke to his chest. As she let Collin wrap her up, Delaney suddenly remembered what security felt like. The snow fell all around them and melted when it hit the water. The two of them just stood there, remembering what it felt like to be in each other's arms.

"I am sorry I left, Collin. I am sorry I didn't trust you enough to know that everything would be okay," Delaney whispered.

"I know, and I am sorry too, for so many things."

Delaney hesitated before she spoke again. "It was about a month after my grandma Ginny passed away that I ran across my mother's old journals.

They were in the attic of Grandma's old house in Sherwood."

"I loved that house," Collin said, "we took lots of walks out there during your grandma's Fourth of July picnics."

Delaney smiled at Collin. "Yes, I remember." Her story was about to take a dark turn, and she snuggled closer into Collin, not just for his physical warmth.

"I know it was not my place to look through my mother's personal things, but I thought my mom and I were so close. I thought I knew everything about her. But the journals dated back to 1989, when my mom was a senior in high school." Delaney stopped to take a breath and then continued before she lost her nerve. "What I read in those diaries about broke my heart. My mom found out that she was pregnant her senior year. When she tells the story in the journal, she says she went to her father. He told her he had a solution and they would take care of it. He took her to a local Planned Parenthood clinic. I didn't even know Planned Parenthood existed back then. My mom described the whole thing, and I read it word for word. Collin, when I found out I was pregnant, I freaked out. We had just graduated. You had these big dreams of taking over your father's firm someday, and I was gonna be the first female CEO of my dad's company. We were going be a power couple—the dream team. And in my mind, I ruined it all."

"That is not the truth, Delaney."

"I know Collin, just let me finish. I was scared. The whole week after I found out was miserable. I even thought about taking my own life. But, I kept thinking about the baby. I convinced myself that our parents would want me to end the life growing inside of me. And I had already grown attached! I did not want to dishonor my family or yours, but I did not want to end the life of my baby either. So, I started saving my money, and I decided that as soon as I started showing even a hint, I would run. I packed up the few pairs of stretchy pants and shirts I owned and bolted across the state, not even looking back. My hormones were crazy, so I think I cried every day for the first month I was gone. But then, I resolved that I could do this, and that Delaney Evans was strong and could make it on her own." She was crying again. "That was right and wrong at the same time. I made it, but it sucked. I missed you so much, Collin. And I missed my parents like crazy too! And now I wonder if they will ever take me back."

"Delaney," said Collin, "I should let you know. Your parents have not been the same since you left."

"How so?" Delaney inquired with a puzzled look on her face.

"Well, I haven't spoken with them in months, and you know how the ladies at church talk—so my mom has shared things with me a couple of times when I called home. She said your mom had been battling depression and that your dad is relying on others too much at the office. I've been worried about them and I pray for them often. I have thought a lot about it. If I was as miserable as I have been—and I didn't even want to live without you—well, they are your parents. How much more hopeless and broken are they feeling?"

"I need to talk to them, Collin. As a matter of fact, I need to talk to them today. Would you like to come to my house with me and meet Dr. Winters? She is the surgeon who saved Riley's life. She has fed and clothed us for the last month. And I also have a hunch that she even paid all of Riley's doctor bills at the hospital where she works. Although, I don't think she would ever admit it."

"I would love to!" Collin said, with genuine desire to meet this woman.

Then Delaney said, "I have a phone call to make. Maybe you can hang out with Riley while I talk to my parents."

"Sounds great, Delaney. But one more thing first."

Collin tried to still his heartbeat. "Delaney, I don't know what I would do without you. And I don't know how I survived without you for this long. But I do know this: I don't ever want to be apart again, and I want to know my son. I want to be little Riley's daddy. And, Delaney Evans—"

Collin got down on one knee right there in the snow on that little Grapeview beach front. "Delaney, I don't want to live without you. I know we have not done everything right. And I know I am far from perfect, but I want to spend the rest of my life making up for the time that we have lost. Delaney Marie Evans, will you marry me? Our parents are probably going to freak out, but we are going to have to trust God to work that part out. Our love is powerful and it will last forever; I do not want to spend another day without you! You are so special to me and I—"

Delaney reached down and set her hand over Collins mouth. "If you would stop talking now, I have something to say."

Collin kissed the inside of her palm and then took her hand back into his. "What, my love, what do you say? Will you marry me?"

"Yes, Collin Riley Haggerty, I will marry you. And I would love nothing more than for you to get to know your son!"

Collin rose to his feet, took Delaney in his arms, and kissed her. He kissed her like he had been dreaming of doing for the last 18 months.

"Oh, I almost forgot." Collin reached into his pocket and pulled out a small box. He took the beautiful ring out of the box and slipped it on Delaney's finger.

"It is beautiful Collin, thank you!"

"I love you, Delaney. I wondered if I could ever truly be happy again. I can assure you, I am so happy right now! Oh, and one more thing." Collin pulled the coffee card out of his pocket and handed it to Delaney.

"What is this, Collin?"

"Well, that was just in case you weren't happy to see me and I had to work a little harder to get the yes from you. Thanks for making that so easy." Delaney laughed and Collin was simply beaming. "Now, future Mrs. Haggerty, you have a phone call to make!"

Delaney spoke softly as she took one more look at the ring on her finger. "I will never again miss talking to my parents on Christmas." They joined hands and headed back up to the James' house to say goodbye. They hated to cut their visit short, but they knew the James family would completely understand.

Chapter 22

Jessica walked back into the living room to find Franklin and Dolores sitting on her sofa, holding hands. They were the portrait of a perfectly loving couple. Jessica's mind wondered about the circumstances that had led them to this place.

"I talked to my friend I was telling you about, and she is going to get the message to Delaney. She is going to do it very gently so as to not spook her into not coming back to my home. Delaney seems to be a very independent girl. She has been working for me as my housekeeper and cook, and she does an amazing job. You have raised a wonderful, respectful, and hardworking daughter, Mr. and Mrs. Evans. Many of us have grown to love her here."

Dolores spoke up. "I just don't understand why she left Tigard. We have a beautiful home, and she never wanted for anything. I cannot even imagine how she has survived all of this time. I really thought that in the end, it would be money that brought her back home. I cannot imagine it has been easy for her the past 18 months. Forgive me if it is hard for me to imagine my little princess working as a maid."

Franklin thought of the credit card Delaney had in her purse, and decided now was not the time to explain how he had kept its existence from his wife. She had all but ordered him to close the account weeks after Delaney left. They had agreed to leave her cell phone operational no matter what, until they found that Delaney had simply not taken her phone with her. The location tracking app that came with their phone plan was no good to them at all.

Mr. Franklin spoke for the first time since they had arrived at Jessica's beach house. "The only thing I can think of, is she had had a fight with her boyfriend Collin. But whenever I talked to the boy, his adamancy that he had no clue where Delaney was seemed nothing but genuine."

"Delaney was spending so much time with that boy before and after graduation that she gave up most of her other friends. But that did not keep me from contacting the ones I used to see her with," Dolores added. "The more we searched, the more we hit one dead end after another."

Tears formed in the woman's eyes and Jessica handed her a box of tissues.

"Do you have any insight as to what brought Delaney to Belfair?" Franklin asked Jessica. For a moment, Jessica did not say anything; she just thought about how on earth to answer. Jessica knew exactly what brought Delaney to Belfair. She was just unsure how Delaney had come to the conclusion that her parents would not have accepted her pregnancy. Somehow, there had to be more to the story. Jessica was very curious to find out what the missing piece to the puzzle was.

Chapter 23

Delaney walked into the James' house hand in hand with Collin. Riley was sitting at the dining room table with Blake by his side. His face was covered in chocolate cream pie.

"It is easier to say 'I am sorry' than to ask for permission sometimes," Blake said to Delaney in a sweet yet questioning voice. Delaney couldn't help but laugh out loud. Blake handed her a container of wipes that were sitting on the floor next to the table and Delaney began to wash off Riley's face. Delaney reached to take the plate of pie away from Riley and as clear as a bell, the little boy said, "No."

Delaney looked at Collin and then at Blake. "I think you two have just witnessed Riley's first word."

"Really?" Collin said, looking like he would burst.

"Well, I am so glad I could inspire that for you," Blake said with a little more spunk in his voice this time. Collin laughed and took the plate from Delaney and put it in the sink.

John walked into the dining room to see what all the commotion was, took one look at Riley, and knew Blake was the culprit.

"From one pie lover to another, right son?" John asked, tussling Blake's hair.

"Yep," said Blake with satisfaction. "Man, I knew there was something great about that kid."

"Well guys," said Delaney, "we are actually going to head back to Jessica's house a little earlier than I had expected. After reconnecting with Collin today and talking about some important things, I started wondering how my parents are. I feel like I need to talk to them. I know that I made a mistake, leaving Oregon when I did. And it's time to face the mess I made. My parents may not even want to talk to me. I am sure they are hurt and angry, but I have to try."

"Anna, come in here," John called into the play room where Anna was playing with her niece Bella and her nephew Kyle. A third toddler, little Jaden, was asleep on the couch. Anna had been reading books to Bella and Kyle, trying to get them to rest. She rose from her place between the two kids and came into the dining room with a scowl on her face.

"What?" She said, "you're gonna wake the little ones."

"Sorry," John said, "I just wanted to let you know that Collin and Delaney are headed to

Jessica's. Delaney is feeling the need to contact her parents this Christmas."

"Oh wow," said Anna. "That is . . . well . . . great."

"Okay Anna, what's up?" Delaney questioned her. "You are acting a little weird." John and Anna exchanged a look of uncertainty and Collin looked over to Blake.

"Don't look at me, I have no clue what their issue is!" Blake laughed.

"Okay, Delaney and Collin, let's go sit down in the living room for a moment." The group filed out of the dining room, leaving Blake to finish cleaning up Riley.

"I am getting a little nervous here," Delaney confessed.

"The thing is," started Anna, "you have probably all noticed that Jessica never showed up for dinner. She called me a bit ago and told me that—well, your parents are at her house. I was just in the other room trying to think of the best way to tell you."

"How is that even possible?" Delaney exclaimed. "Collin, did you say something to my parents about finding me here?"

"No," Collin said, "I didn't even tell my own parents I found you. I have not told a soul! Well, except Jax, and he said he wouldn't tell anyone."

"I think Jess said something about them driving to the Alderbrook for a vacation and seeing what they were sure was your Jeep parked in her driveway," Anna explained.

"Wow, talk about strange coincidences," said Delaney.

"Totally," Collin said.

"When they went back to the house to see if it was you, Jessica was there. She knew after one glance that your mom was your mom."

"Yes, I always have been a bit of a mini me," said Delaney, smiling. "So, you are telling me that my parents are at Jessica's house waiting for me right now?"

"Yes, that is exactly what I am saying."

"On Christmas?"

"Yes."

"Oh, my." Delaney sat down on the couch, then got right back up. "What are we waiting for? Let's go see my parents!"

"Okay," Collin said readily. Then he turned to John. "John, I have a huge favor to ask. What's the chance that I can leave my car here and come get it later? I don't want to send Delaney out alone and in shock in the snow."

"I can do one better. If you leave me your key, Anna can take our car home and I can drop yours by Jessica's on our way home."

"Wow, that would be great."

"It will be rough, but if you need me to drive that beautiful Mustang GT to you on Christmas, I will do it." Collin laughed.

"It will be like you own little Christmas miracle, Dad," piped up Ben, who had turned the corner just in time to hear the last bit of their conversation. John agreed with Ben, and Collin handed over the key to the car he had received for high school graduation.

"I want one of those for graduation too, Dad," said Ben.

"Good luck with that, son," John said. And with hugs all around, Delaney and Collin were off to meet Delaney's parents.

"Could this day get any stranger?" Delaney said to Collin as she tucked Riley into his car seat.

"I imagine it probably can," Collin said. "I just hope this next reunion goes as great as ours did, because this day has been pretty great so far."

Delaney looked at him with warmth in her eyes. "I love you, Collin. Thanks for finding me. I was even more lost than I thought I was."

Chapter 24

The ride from Grapeview to Jessica's South Shore home was nearly silent, but peaceful. The snow flurries had picked up again, yet the main roads were fairly clear with the temperatures hovering between 33 and 34 degrees. Collin was driving and Delaney only spoke occasionally to give him directions.

The scene was nothing short of magical. It was hard to believe that Delaney was going to see her parents tonight. How had she let this go so long? Delaney fingered the bracelet on her arm that little Brooklyn had picked out for her. She touched the primroses and felt a simple sense of home. She had really grown to love this town, and these people. In Belfair, Delaney grew up. She left childish things behind, needing to raise a child instead. Riley depended on her for everything, and she had done what it took to give him everything he needed.

Delaney suddenly thought back to those nights before Riley was born, when she was big and pregnant. She thought of the women in the mother's shelter where she stayed. Those ladies had shown her unconditional kindness, no questions asked. Then she thought about when she first heard about Riley's diagnosis, and then the surgery. The primroses on her wrist would be her reminder to live life. Life was beautiful; she refused to just let it pass her by.

All of a sudden, they were nearing Jessica's house. Delaney realized she was preparing to walk into a room with people who really didn't know her any more. Delaney was a different person. She was no longer too proud to shop at Goodwill, or buy the milk at the store with the reduced price. Fear began to bring a sense of dread over her. Delaney tried not to give in to the panic that rose in her chest, but before she knew it she could barely breathe.

What if? What if her mother did not accept whom she had become? What if her connection to her was fractured? And what if Collin suddenly discovered that she was not the same girl he knew in Tigard, Oregon? Eighteen months was not a long time, unless you spent it under extreme pressure, fighting for survival, or holding responsibility for the life of a little human fighting for his life. Under those circumstances, eighteen months was a lifetime that created a chasm between two worlds. The air grew thicker. The walls of the car almost seemed to be closing in around Delaney.

Collin looked over, and suddenly he noticed that Delaney did not look well at all. A quick glance behind him confirmed that Riley was totally out, snoozing in the back seat. Collin saw a small turn out on the side of the road. He carefully pulled over.

"Delaney, are you okay?" Collin was starting to get a little scared. The look on Delaney's face reflected terror. "Delaney, what's wrong? Her eyes suddenly welled up. "What's wrong, Laney, are you okay? Talk to me."

In a quiet whisper, Delaney spoke. "What if I have changed too much? I am broken. What if they don't want me?" Now, without invitation, the tears started to fall down Delaney's cheeks. "Collin, I am not the same girl that left Oregon after graduation. I have changed. I have a baby. I shop at Goodwill."

Collin lifted himself slowly onto the middle console between his and Delaney's seats and wrapped his arms around her. "Delaney Marie Evans. You may have changed, you have certainly grown up and matured, but I can tell you this: you have never been more beautiful to me and you have never been more amazing. The intense pressures you have been under have not ruined you. The trials have refined you, pressed you—and like a diamond under pressure, created a treasure. You are still Delaney, but you are stronger than you have ever been. When I saw you the other day, my heart leapt for joy at the possibilities. But tonight, being with you and hearing your heart and seeing everything you have been through, I know I want you more than ever. I want to spend the rest of my life getting to know the strongest, most beautiful, and most resilient girl I know!"

Slowly, Delaney's breathing returned to normal and her heart rate slowed. The terror faded and while Delaney calmed down, Collin held her, sitting in between the seats of a 2014 Jeep Liberty, on Christmas, in the snow. Collin had the feeling that everything was going be okay! The Lord definitely had not brought them this far, only to have them fall apart again. No—God had something special for them. They would still be an amazing future power couple; it would just be a different kind of Power propelling them.

"Delaney, before we go, I think we should pray. What do you think?" Suddenly, Delaney thought about earlier that morning when Jessica had given her that beautiful leather bound study bible. Delaney knew that this God whom Collin had given his life to, whom Anna had been sharing with her over coffee these past weeks—this God who had saved Riley from death just over a month ago, was pursuing her. God wanted Delaney to take that step of faith and decide to follow Him with all her heart. God wanted *all* of her.

"I would really like that, Collin. We may have made some mistakes in the past, but I think trusting God to take us forward in our future would be the rightest thing we have ever done." Then, there in the snow, in the Jeep, with their miracle baby asleep in the backseat, right there on the side of South Shore Road, Collin and Delaney committed their relationship into the hands of Jesus. Delaney, in the silence of her heart, asked Jesus to come into her life for real, and forever.

Anna sat on the sofa curled up with John, watching *It's a Wonderful Life* with everyone. The movie had just begun, but Anna could tell that, even though this was her all-time favorite holiday movie, it was not going to keep her attention tonight. Oh, to be a fly on the wall at Jessica's house tonight! John kept looking over at her and she knew he had to be thinking the same thing. With every five minutes or so that passed, Anna whispered a prayer for Delaney and Collin and Delaney's parents. She really hoped this next meeting would go as well as Delaney's reunion with Collin had gone. Now all they could do was pray!

When the movie was over, the two James families passed around holiday hugs and said their goodbyes. It was time to head home and load up the car for Anna's Christmas trip to the beach tomorrow. As excited as she was, Anna sure hoped she had a chance to talk to Delaney or Jessica before they skipped town tomorrow. All in the course of one day, life in little ol' Belfair had gotten pretty exciting.

Chapter 25

With a sleeping Riley in arms, the newly reconnected couple stood frozen on Jessica's door step. The red poinsettias on Jessica's giant Christmas wreath contrasted sharply with the two inches of snow covering the front porch.

"Well, it's now or never," Delaney said. She was not sure whether it was the fear, the nerves, or the excitement that was in the forefront of her emotional pinwheel. Delaney's state of mind was changing like the wind. She was simply overwrought with feelings. With her hand on the knob, she began to turn it.

As the seal of the door broke, the familiar suction sound filled the silence and the sudden noise brought the eyes of her parents straight to her. There she was, standing in the spacious entryway of the house she had begun to call home, staring at the two of them.

Dolores and Franklin Evans were on their feet at once, rushing towards their only daughter. Then they froze almost as swiftly as they had risen. Jessica was the first one to speak. As she came over to Delaney, she swooped up Riley. "Well, sweetheart, you and your parents have a lot to talk about and this little man is already in dream land.

Let me run him upstairs." And just like that, Riley and Jessica were up the stairs and Delaney was face to face with her parents.

The young woman suddenly found herself wrapped in the biggest, warmest hug from her mother. Then, not waiting for an invitation, Franklin wrapped his arms tightly around his wife and daughter. Collin was unsure exactly what to do with himself, and he was filled with such love for these people in front of him that he thought his heart would explode. The group somehow found their way into the living room of the beach house.

The view from this room was spectacular. As they looked out the wide windows, the snow fell thickly and around the shore, Christmas lights from all of the homes along the water shone like beacons, illuminating the night of Christmas miracles.

"What happened?" Dolores spoke up first. "I am afraid I really don't understand. Unless . . ." Then the realization hit, and there it was all at once.

"Yes, Mother, I got pregnant. I had a baby. That is why I left." Delaney watched her parents' faces, looking for the shock and horror she knew would come. She braced for the disapproval, for the disappointment. But she did not see condemnation. She saw care and concern; she even believed she saw compassion in her mother's eyes, but absolutely no judgment. In the eyes of her father, she saw brokenness, sadness, and possibly some regret. He was not, however, angry. He was hurt.

"Why did you leave, Delaney?" Her father looked at her, pleading for an answer. "We would have helped you figure out your problem."

"Daddy, I am so sorry. But you see, I guess I got scared because I didn't see Riley as a problem to be solved. I saw my situation as a mistake I had made, and the little life I carried inside of me was the innocent bystander along for the ride. He did not need to be solved. He needed a chance to live.

"I don't think I understand what you are saying." Her father spoke the question.

"I do," Dolores spoke up. Then Delaney knew for a fact that her mother knew exactly why she had left.

"Mom, Dad, I was your baby—your little girl. I did not want to disappoint you. I knew you might see my situation as a problem to be solved. There were so many times, Mom, that I almost came to you. And then one day, I was up in Grandma's attic not long after she passed away. It was so interesting up there. It was like wandering through your past, Mom! Grandma had kept so many of your old things. Like prom dresses and old year books. And, she kept all of your old diaries."

Dolores Evans went ashen. Her color drained as her eyes widened. Delaney continued her story.

"I was about eight weeks along or so when I found them. And it was those dusty old books that made me understand exactly what I had to do. I was so scared. But up in that old attic, I began to devise a plan. I knew what I needed to do and I had to make it happen."

Now Dolores was crying freely. "I am so sorry, honey. I would never have even considered sending you down the path that I went down when I was a teenager. I was so young and so scared."

"It's okay, Mom, you don't have to—"

"It's fine, sweetheart. Your father knows the whole story. If it had not been for him, I would probably not be here. I was ready to end it all before we had you, back when your dad and I believed we would never be able to have children. I was terrified that he would find out that I killed a baby. I had so much guilt for ending that little life that I simply did not know what to do with myself. When the doctor told us our infertility issues were because of my past, I had to tell Frank the whole story. I was so ashamed, but your dad helped me work through the pain and the guilt and eventually, I forgave myself. Then a couple years later, I found out I was pregnant with you. You were the only baby we would ever conceive. You were our Christmas miracle, all those years ago. We found out we were pregnant in December and then in late August you came to join our little family. I always hoped you could have a little sibling, but we were never again able to conceive. For years I thought I was being punished for what I had done, that I was inept. Then I let go of the dream of another baby and poured everything I had into being the best mother to you that I could. Raising you seemed effortless. You were so easy, so sweet. You were obedient, studious, and kind. You had awesome potential, big dreams . . . then you were gone."

"I am so sorry, Mom. I was somehow convinced that you would be embarrassed by my problem, and that abortion would be the logical solution. I read about how awful your abortion had been. I read about how empty you felt afterwards. And then, I made my plan to run. And Collin, I was so scared I would ruin you and keep you from your dreams."

Collin looked lovingly at Delaney. Mr. and Mrs. Evans had almost forgotten he was there. "Collin, I knew your parents would hate me, so I had to run far away. I had to say goodbye to everyone so I didn't ruin any of you."

"Oh, Delaney," her mother said, taking her hand. "I am so sorry."

Franklin Evans was speechless. He simply did not have words to describe the way his heart was breaking. The tears left tracks down his cheeks. Turning toward her father, Delaney's heart broke too.

"Daddy, I am sorry! You were the hardest to leave. I knew you would not understand. Yet, I knew you had not completely stopped loving me, because you did not completely close me down. Thank you—I would not have made it without you."

Suddenly, Dolores looked a little confused. "You never closed that ridiculous credit card, did you?" Franklin's eyes turned from pained to a little sheepish.

"No, Dory, I did not. I couldn't. It was my only link to our little girl. And she rarely used it so I watched it like a hawk, attempting to keep a trail of where she had been. That credit card is what led me to Belfair. That card gave me hope that I could find Delaney so that I could bring you back to me as well." The look of love that filled Dolores eyes touched Frank's heart. They shared a moment there in that room. It said, *we are gonna make it; we won't give up on each other.*

As if struck, Franklin looked abruptly over at Collin. "So, what exactly is your story? How on earth did you find Delaney before I did?"

"Well that, sir, was nothing other than the handiwork of God." Collin then proceeded to tell the Evans how he had ended up in Belfair; how he had found Jesus; and how he had never given up on the hope that he would find his one and only love.

As they continued talking the night away, they were suddenly interrupted by the sound of crying. Delaney ran up to Riley's room to find Jessica attempting to calm the little boy.

"He wants his mamma," Jess said with a sleepy smile. It was 2:00 a.m. and Riley still awoke once a night at around this time to nurse. He was almost ready to be weaned, but after he had been so frighteningly ill, it was one comfort Delaney had let her sweet little man hold on to. She sat down in the small nursery holding little Riley, wrapped in his handmade afghan that had been bundled in prayer, and nursed her son.

Hearing footsteps ascending the stairs, Delaney looked in the doorway to see her mother peeking in, watching her in this special moment with her son.

"Can I come in?" Dolores spoke softly.

"Of course you can. There is only one chair, but my bed is in the corner there and you are welcome to sit on it." As she sat down on her daughter's bed in a room that was so foreign to her, Dolores once again could not hold back tears.

"I am sure going to look like a mess tomorrow," she said.

"Won't we all?" Delaney replied.

"Delaney, I am so sorry that you did not feel like you could come to us when you found yourself in such a predicament. I can't believe I am a grandma . . ." Her voice trailed off.

Delaney smiled. "He is almost done. Then you can hold him."

Downstairs, Collin sat with Mr. Franklin Evans. The rich, powerful, and intimidating Franklin Evans. Collin mustered up a voice, looked up and said, "Mr. Evans, I don't know if this is a good time—in fact, I don't know if there will ever be a good time—but I have something I need to ask you." He cleared his throat and continued. "Sir, I am deeply and hopelessly in love with you daughter. And . . . well . . . sir, I would love your permission to marry her."

Franklin smiled at Collin. "You know what, young man, I have always liked you. I honestly could not see anyone else being good enough for my baby girl, and as terrified as I am to be a grandfather, I can say that I am very excited to be a father-in-law. Dory and I always wanted a son, and we could have never asked for a better, kinder, and more deserving one than you. So, when are you going to pop the question? You should make it soon since, well, you are already a father!"

"Actually, sir, I popped the question several hours ago and she said yes, if it was okay with you. So I am getting married! I am thinking maybe even on New Year's Day. You know, new year, new beginning!"

"Wow, Mr. Haggerty, you don't waste any time."

"I have lost too much time already, sir, and I don't want to waste another day!"

"I can respect that," Franklin said. Then the two men talked more about life and the shock of being a dad and a grandpa, and then a little bit more about the Seahawks and their hopes for the Super Bowl.

Dolores looked down into the smiling face of her first grandbaby.

"He is so beautiful. He is such a perfect mix of you and Collin."

"I know, isn't he?" Delaney smiled at her little man. "Mom, there is something I haven't told you yet, but I feel like I need to tell you and Dad together. Would you mind if we went back downstairs?"

"Of course, sweetheart," Dolores said as she followed Delaney out of the room.

Once downstairs, Delaney began her speech. "Mom, Dad, there is one more thing I need to tell you guys about your grandson. Riley had congenital heart failure. He was probably born with it, but almost didn't make it a couple months back. If it had not been for the skilled hand of Jessica Winters, he would not be with us. I just wanted you to know what a miracle he is. I know that things should have gone a lot differently with the birth of this little guy. I do, however, believe that I ended up in Belfair for a reason. I know I needed to meet Jessica and I know that God brought my other new friend Anna into my life for a reason. You see, if it had not been for those two ladies I would not have found my new faith in Jesus. I am not the same as I used to be, and I know it will take some getting used to, but I know God has a plan for me and Riley—and I think for me and Collin as well." She smiled. "In a week, Collin and I are getting married. And Mom and Dad, I hope you will be there."

"As if we would miss it," said Franklin, smiling at his wife.

"I want to get married here in Belfair. I feel like this is my place of new beginnings, new life. And Collin, I know we have a lot to talk about, but I want you to know that I don't want to leave Belfair. I feel like this where I want to raise little Riley, and he has great medical care here. I found Jesus here, and I feel like I have support and roots."

Riley had his fingers all wound up in the afghan and Delaney thought again about her beginnings here in this little town. She was suddenly overwhelmed with love for her community and all its people. Even with its pot shops on every corner, Belfair was her new home.

Chapter 26

"Oh Billy Joe McGuffey was a really clumsy kid

On the third day of third grade I'll tell you what he did . . ."

Only nine more verses and this song would finally be over. How did the kids have this and a hundred other crazy songs just floating around in their heads? Anna laughed silently as they entered Aberdeen, Washington. Not long now and she would be relaxing in front of her window, listening to waves crash in the surf. That morning Delaney had called her and updated her on the whole story. The most exciting part was that Delaney and Riley were staying in Belfair, at least for a while. And she and Collin were getting married in just a week! Anna was honored that Delaney and Collin had asked her to perform the ceremony and lead them in their vows. There would be so much to do when she got back! But there were three days to spend at the beach first.

Collin had returned to Oregon to spend the night with his parents and share his future plans with his family. Delaney had made Anna promise to pray continuously for Collin as he shattered his parents' dreams for their son's future, for the second time. Poor Collin. She would be praying for the best.

Delaney was spending the next two days reconnecting with her parents, going to the spa, and planning a wedding. They were all staying at the Alderbrook, but Anna was sure there would be several trips into Silverdale in the near future as they pulled together a wedding in a week. It was a good thing that the Evans saw money as no object, because *last minute* and *cheap* were not two words that usually accompanied each other in wedding descriptions.

John pulled into the Aberdeen Starbucks and threatened the kids if they did not hush while he ordered a coffee for each of them. John got each child a Caramel Frappuccino, and while they enjoyed them, the car was filled with glorious silence. Anna secretly had to admit, though, that she loved the sweet sound of her kiddos singing.

A grande Pike Roast with light ice in her hand, on her way to the beach—did it get any better than this? Not to mention, John had sprung for her favorite hotel. Anna loved the Best Western because of the lighthouse in the middle of the hotel. Rain or shine, she loved to go up those stairs and look out at the water. There were few things more relaxing than the beach!

As they entered the hotel and walked up to the front counter, John pulled out his ID and credit card. He handed it to the young lady at the counter and suddenly, the woman looked a little shocked.

"I am afraid that we have accidentally given away your room." Anna's heart dropped as she wondered in dismay what they were going to do. "But," the lady continued, "just a moment. I am going to see what I can do. I am afraid, however, that we may have all of our rooms booked for the night." Anna said a little prayer under her breath and John did the same as he waited for the young woman to come back.

She returned promptly. "Well, the bummer is that we do not have any regular rooms left, but if you are willing to make a little upgrade, we do have our suite available for the four days that you are here."

"How much extra is that going to cost us?" John asked, wanting to make it work but knowing they were on a very tight budget. Just then, an older gentleman walked over to the counter and joined the conversation.

"Jaime," he said to the young receptionist, "this was our mistake and we will make it right. Mr.—" He paused for a moment to look down at the reservation screen. ". . . James," he said, "the larger room will be made available to you at no extra charge."

"Wow, thank you sir!" John said. "We really appreciate it."

"It is our pleasure," said the older man, *Matt* his name tag read.

"Thank you again, Matt." John said to him. "This is wonderful. Thank you, and God bless you both."

"And God bless you as well, Mr. James," replied Jaime with a smile.

"Oh, he definitely has." John finished signing the paperwork and then the James family headed up to their room. They were greeted by a giant picture window, a beautiful balcony, a fire place, a hot tub, and the biggest bonus of all—they could not just hear the waves, but they could see them!

"Wow," John said as he headed into the room. "This is beautiful." The kids even had their own separate sleeping quarters. "This may turn out to be the best beach trip ever," He said to Anna with a wink. "I cannot wait to test out that hot tub."

"Thank you, God, for giving us more than we expect," Anna whispered in prayer. "You always take care of us."

"This room is great!" Ben exclaimed as he threw his bags down on the bed and ran to the balcony, throwing open the glass door. "Can we go to the pool?"

"Whoa, hold it, boss. Can we unpack first?"

"I am gonna go jogging while you guys swim," Blake said as he dug in his bag for a stocking cap. "I am sure there is some gorgeous girl out there, just waiting to be impressed by all of *this*," he said, gesturing down his body.

"In your dreams," Ben said with a scoff. "You know you want to come to the pool. There could be girls there, ya know."

"Please come swim with us, Blake," Brooklyn said in her sweetest 'I love you' voice.

"Fine," said Blake, "the beach can wait." And with that, the James family unpacked and headed to the pool. Anna just knew this was going to be a fabulous few days.

Chapter 27

Collin pulled his Mustang into the driveway of his parents' beautiful, 8,000-square-foot brick home. He felt the bumps on the cobblestone circle at the front entrance and had a sudden mental flash back. He had spent so many hours riding his bike over the bumpy stones, pretending he was Jeff Gordon in his trusty #24 car. He would pretend he was in Martinsville racing with the best of the best. He could smell the exhaust and see the fans in the grandstands surrounding the track.

Those were the good ol' days. Such a beautiful home he had grown up in. So many memories were made here in this place, memories of times when life seemed so much simpler. So many evenings spent here dreaming of the future, his future with Delaney Evans.

The amber glow of at least twenty porch lights illuminated his view as he parked near the last of the garage doors. Collin could not even begin to fathom how Delaney had spent Riley's first several months living in her car. It was all still so unreal. He pushed the button affixed to his visor and the garage door began to lift. He pulled the Mustang into the wide open room that his father had specifically given to him the day he got his first car. For a minute, Collin just sat in his car after he closed the garage behind him and cut the engine. *Collin Haggerty, you are a father now*, he thought to himself. Now it was time to go and break the news to his parents and hope that at the same time, he did not break their hearts.

It was now or never. Collin walked down the corridor from the garage that led into the main part of his childhood home. His mother was sitting on a small floral print love seat with her ear to her phone. She held up one finger to Collin with a big smile on her face, gesturing that she would just be one more minute on her phone call. Collin felt small arms suddenly around his waist and he turned around to see his younger sister Cara with a smile that warmed his heart. His sister was stunning, just like his mother. Petite with gorgeous blonde hair, and just a smattering of freckles along her nose, Cara was the picture of the perfect high-schooler. She was, however, looking a little bit on the overly thin side these days. Cara was turning eighteen in two days and graduating from high school—my, how time had flown.

Cara and Collin had always been close, until the day Delaney disappeared and Collin pulled away from everyone. He felt like this year, while he was at school, he had managed to partially mend his relationship with his little sister by making sure to call her each week and hanging out with her on the weekends that he came home. Being an only child, Delaney had loved Cara like a little sister. Cara had idolized Delaney. And when she disappeared without a trace, Cara had been heart broken.

Collin had no idea how Cara would take all the crazy news that he was about to deliver, and he was nervous. Cara was missing something very important in her life, and that was Jesus. During the last year and a half Cara had turned into a bit of a wild child. She has become an animal advocate, a vegan, and a woman's right activist, all in the course of eighteen months. Collin had made a vow to himself during one late-night prayer and jam session with his buddies that he would always be there for Cara and he would always work to show her the love of Jesus with everything inside him.

"Hey, little sis," he reached out and hugged Cara tight. "I missed you. How was Christmas?"

"Awful," Cara said with an over-exaggerated eye roll. "I had to spend the day knowing there was a giant bird carcass blistering inside our stove. Mom and Dad bickered the whole day and, well, without you here, it really sucked! Mom was tipsy by six o'clock and that made everything even more miserable. Do I dare ask you how your holiday was?"

Collin's stomach did a full somersault inside his body at the thought of his miraculous Christmas.

"How is Jax?" Cara asked with a smile. His baby sister had had a crush on his best friend for years.

"Still two years older than you."

"Whatever, it's only nineteen months. Tell me all about your dirt biking adventure. Where did you guys go again? Talula?"

"Tahuya," Collin corrected. "They have some seriously awesome trails up there. We camped out in a little town called Belfair. It was right on the Hood Canal. It was really beautiful. I will tell you all about it when Mom gets off the phone."

"Fine. Until then, why don't you describe how Jax looked in his riding pants!"

"That is so gross," Collin said, lightly punching his sister in the arm.

"Oh, he is so hot, and I never see him anymore now that you are gone."

"Cara, you are hopeless. You know Jax is not into dating right now. He wants to finish school first and you, my dear, are still in high school, so dream on. Plus, I thought you were totally not into that Jesus thing? Oh, and you should also know—Jax eats his double cheeseburgers smothered in bacon."

"Oh shut up, you jerk. You know that for a little attention from the gorgeous Jax Jefries, I might show my face in church once in a while. Hey, big bro—that is not such a bad idea. Maybe if I found a suddenly liked Jesus, I might get to sit by that amazing specimen on Sunday morning in the pew! Hey, and don't you guys hold hands and sing Kumbaya while you pray? I can just feel our sweat mingle now. I am never washing this hand again," Cara said dramatically as she spun around holding her hand to her chest.

"Oh my goodness, Cara, does the word *pathetic* mean anything to you?" But in his heart, Collin was really thinking Jax would not get near his sister with a ten foot pole unless she sold out to Jesus. On the other hand, if Jax was what it took to get his sister into the doors of a church, let the games begin.

Just then, Collin heard the door to the den open and out walked Collin's father. Large in stature, Carter Haggerty filled the room with his presence the way he filled his courtrooms with fear. Carter had an air about him that even his children were intimidated by. At that same moment, Collin's mother Lacey hung up the phone and came to stand by her husband.

"Son, I am glad you made it home safely," said Carter. Collin suddenly wondered how he was going to tell his parents about all that had happened that weekend.

"Dinner should be ready in about ten minutes," continued Lacey. "We will be eating in the formal dining room tonight. I thought that would be nice, Collin, since you missed the beautiful Christmas duck Marta prepared for us on Christmas." Collin looked over and smiled at his sister, who glared at him in return.

"I am sure it was delicious."

"Oh, and tonight she made your favorite baked macaroni and grilled tri tip roast. I think I gained five pounds just smelling it for the last two hours."

Lacey Haggerty put her hand on her stomach, as if to hide the pounds that simply were not there. If nothing else, Collin's mother had kept her figure impeccably over the years. She was a beautiful woman, thin, with beautiful long strawberry blonde curls. She neither looked nor dressed her fifty-three years of age. But she had a hidden sadness in her eyes that Collin wished he could take away. It was not easy being Carter Haggerty's wife. He should know, because he often hated being Carter Haggerty's son. And before he had found hope in Jesus, Collin often wondered if he would be just like this man someday. But now, he prayed his parents would find what he had found. Suddenly, Collin knew that God had a plan. God knew that as long as Collin saw Delaney as his "savior," he would never know the deep need he had for a *true* Savior, the Savior of his soul.

Marta walked into the room in her adorable white frilled apron, the one Collin knew his mother desired her to wear in order for the family to put on a certain image. Collin loved Marta. She had been cooking and cleaning for his family for about twelve years, and she knew just what he liked. He remembered spending hours as a kid sitting on a stool in the kitchen talking to Marta about life and, in his high school years, about love. Marta was the one who had encouraged him to talk to Jax about going to church. And after he gave his heart to Jesus, she prayed for him to have the courage to talk to his father about going to Northwest University. Marta had been widowed for ten years and had a daughter who must be about 30 by now.

She had always seemed to have plenty of time for Collin. She would always try to hunt him down and say goodnight before she headed to her little house in McMinnville each night. She would always save him extra chocolate chip cookies or brownies, which were his favorites, and leave them on his night table by his bed. What would Marta think when he her told her he was a father?

"Mr. Collin, I am so glad you are home for a visit. You have been missed," Marta said.

"Thank you, Marta, I hear dinner is going to be delightful."

"Yes, sir," she said, "and I made brownies."

Dinner was quiet, but not too uncomfortable. As much as Collin loved the food on his plate, it was sitting in his stomach like a rock. Collin knew his time here was limited and he need to get things said. And so, out it came.

"I found Delaney on Christmas. I don't know why I never went looking for her, but there she was in little Belfair."

The room was silent. Collin could hear the ticking of the large clock on the wall as his family just stared at him.

"Did you talk to her?" Cara was the first to break the silence.

"Yes," Collin said. "And she did a lot of explaining. I now understand what happened and why Delaney ran. She simply felt like it was all she could do."

"I am confused," said Cara. "Why did she leave? That makes no sense."

Collin let it erupt like a baking soda volcano. He spewed his story out at the dinner table. "It was prom night and things went too far. It only happened once, but once is all it took. Mom, Dad, I am a father to a beautiful little man named Riley Franklin. You are grandparents and Cara, you are an aunt."

Without saying a word, Collin's father stood up and walked out of the room, taking most of the oxygen with him.

"Oh, honey," Lacey said, looking torn between turning to Collin or going after her husband. In the end she, too, walked out of the room.

"Holy crap, this is rich! First Bible college, and now a baby." Cara had a crazy look on her face. "You are gonna send our father to an early grave.

You really don't have to work so hard to ruin your perfect son image."

Collin didn't know whether to laugh or cry at his sister's candid reaction.

"Well wait, if you think *that* is too much, Delaney and I are getting married on New Year's."

"Ok, you are kidding me?" Cara said. "I still can't believe you're a dad. You can't even do your own laundry. You are a dad. And now you're getting hitched. I have now heard it all."

Lacey stood in the doorway of her husband's den, standing on ground she had never walked upon. She had no idea what she was supposed to do in a situation like this. Carter was not a man who liked to lose, especially when it came to losing control. And right now, he had lost everything.

Carter had hoped that his son would come around, that he would give up on these ridiculous ideas of being a pastor. He was lawyer material. He had been groomed for a career in law since preschool! Where had he gone wrong? Collin was his hope; he was the one who would live out his father's dream. But now, with a baby, this would make things very difficult. He hoped to God that Collin would not get a crazy notion to marry this girl. That would ruin everything! What was he going to do? If he had known about the baby sooner, he could have talked some sense into Delaney. Her parents were sensible; Franklin and Dolores had been good friends with the Haggertys before Delaney disappeared. They could have taken care of things quietly, terminating the problem.

"Are you okay, Carter?" Lacey was standing in the doorway. A sense of failure came over Carter at that moment.

"Please go away," Carter said.

"I am so sorry, Carter."

"Go away!" Carter yelled and began to stand to his feet. "I am sure this is your fault somehow, Lacey, you made him soft. All that praying you did for him when he was little. Get out of my sight."

Lacey turned away and walked toward her room. Carter knew how to be cruel. He knew how to use words to wound. But right now, in this moment, even though Carter's harshness was painful, Lacey Haggerty wondered if her prayers for her son when he was a baby had been the one right thing she had ever done for him. And right there in her room, Lacey Haggerty got down on her knees and prayed for her son, for Delaney, and for this new development—her grandson. Then Lacey said a prayer for her husband. "Dear God, I am so sorry I let intimidation cause me to abandon my childhood faith, but right now, my husband needs help. In his stubborn pride, he will allow his broken heart to be the death of our family. Lord, somehow in the midst of it all, let Carter find you. Amen." And with that, Lacey stood up, dried her eyes, and marched back out to the dining room to hug her firstborn son. It had been too long since she acted like the mother she needed to be. But Lacey knew it was not too late.

When Collin saw his mother, he could tell she had been crying, but he saw her smile from behind her overwhelmed tears. Lacey came over and wrapped her arms around her son. She told him that she was sorry for not doing this sooner and Collin felt the tears fill the rims of his own eyes. His mother looked up at him just as those tears he was trying to stop released from his eyes and fell down his face.

"Oh mom, I am so sorry I have disappointed you. I have a little more to tell you. Delaney and I are getting married. Not because we think it is the right thing to do, but because we love each other and neither one of us wants to live another day without each other. And then there is little Riley; he is going to need a daddy. I am going to finish up this semester at Northwest, but I will do it as a married man."

"Oh Collin, are you sure?"

"Yes, Mom, I am completely sure. We are getting married on New Year's Day."

"Like now?" His mother asked bewildered, "like, less than a week away?"

"Yes," Collin said, "in Belfair. Will you come? I can't imagine getting married without my family there."

"Of course I will be there. But I can't answer for your father; he is pretty upset. But we can pray he changes his mind!"

"Pray?" Collin said. "Did you actually say we should pray for him?"

"Oh, Collin, I have so much to tell you, to explain to you, and to apologize for. Jesus and I— we used to be close. But I gave up my faith for an image. As your father's practice began to soar and he became the number one criminal law firm in the greater Portland area, your father saw my faith as an unneeded crutch. If I depended on God, I didn't need him, he said. One day, I chose your father over my faith and the rest is history. Tonight, the Lord and I made things right. And you can expect my full support from here on out. As for your father, he is going to need a lot of prayer."

"I cannot believe what I am hearing here," interjected Cara suddenly. "Golden boy over here is most likely gonna drop out of university, and he knocked up some girl, and you are crying and hugging? When do we start singing Kumbaya? I can't believe this," Cara said. "But if we are all headed to Belfair, I am in. You are not leaving me here with the monster grump that dad is sure to be. When do we leave?"

"I am leaving tomorrow at noon," explained Collin. "And I would love it if you guys came too."

John and Anna sat off to the side of the pool. Anna was pretending to read a novella on her Kindle while John played tetris on his phone. The boys were swimming and showing off for a couple of cute sisters who were sitting in the hot tub, and Brooke had made a quick friend of a little girl who was about a year younger than she. Anna had the strangest feeling in her gut as she sat there in the pool seat, and she put down her Kindle in her lap and began to pray.

Anna started praying for Delaney and little Riley, but that was not where her burden was coming from. Anna then began to pray for Collin and his parents. She knew this could not be easy on them. Collin had shared with John before they had left the James' house on Christmas that his parents were not believers, and that they still hoped for Collin to become some big top-notch lawyer. Anna prayed for the delivery of the news Collin would be giving and she prayed for acceptance and love to fill their house. And above all, Anna prayed that Collin Haggerty's family would find Jesus.

This has to be done, Collin thought as he stood at his father's doorway and knocked. There was no answer, so Collin let himself in. What he saw broke his heart. His father had tear stains on his face.

"Dad," Collin said, "I am so sorry. I know I made a mistake that I cannot go back and fix, but I love Delaney. I want to know my son. I want to see his first steps and hear him say 'daddy'. I asked Delaney to marry me. We are getting married on January 1st, New Year's Day. It would mean the world to me if you were there. And I hope you will be okay with Mom coming with me tomorrow. I know this is what I need to do."

Carter looked up at his son. "Collin Haggerty," he growled, "if you walk out that door tomorrow and you go through with this ludicrous plan to end your life by walking down that aisle, you and I are finished. You will also not see another penny of my money. That is your choice. I believe I raised you to be smarter than this. The choice is yours."

Collin was hearing the exact words he had expected to hear. He was not, however, hearing the words he had hoped to hear. "Father, I love you. I respect the strong, successful man you are. However, in this situation, you are wrong. On New Year's Day, I will not end my life. I will start fresh with a beautiful new beginning. And I hope with everything inside me that you will be there to celebrate this new beginning with me."

A cold smile crossed over Carter's Haggerty's face. "When hell freezes over, you will see me in that church. I don't care what your mother does. She is weak and always has been. Howbeit, all the same, I will not be there."

"Once again, Dad, you are wrong. Mom is one of the strongest women I know. Sometimes strength is simply silence." And with that, Collin Haggerty walked out his father's mahogany den door and out of his father's life for what might be forever. Yet, no matter how long it took, Collin would continue to pray for his father's salvation. Despite his father's harshness and tough love, he loved his father very much. Deep inside, he knew his father loved him too, but just had a difficult time expressing it.

Heading to his room, Collin did not think he could sleep. He sat down and wrote his mom and sister a note after they slipped off to bed. He explained that he needed to head back and see Delaney. He left them directions to get to Delaney's house in Belfair, Washington, and told them he was staying at the Day's Inn in Port Orchard, a town close to Belfair. Collin told them he would see them as soon as they worked it out to get there. He walked over to his night stand to put the letter there, where he knew his mother was sure to find it, and saw the brown paper sack with a note taped to it. He opened the note. It was from Marta.

I noticed you did not get to finish your supper, so I made you a snack. Just heat it in the microwave for a minute. And there are brownies for you, too.

P.S. Your father will come around. I will be praying he does.

Warmest regards,

Marta.

Picking up the paper sack and leaving his note in its place, Collin went out, got in his car, and drove away from his beautiful childhood home, wondering if his own child would ever be welcomed there, praying for one more miracle.

A quick phone call later, Collin had one more stop to make. He turned off in the direction of Sherwood. He needed to talk to Jax tonight; he needed some wisdom that he hoped his old buddy would have for him. Collin also thought he might need to give his friend a heads up to run the other way if his sister Cara ever set foot in Jax's church.

When he arrived at Jax's house, he took the brownies out of the bag and left them on the seat of the car. When Jax answered the door, Collin tossed Jax the bag of mac and cheese and said one word: "Marta."

"Yes!" Jax rejoiced, "I have not had Marta's cooking in forever! Jesus loves me, man." Collin laughed weakly, and Jax led him into his family room. They had a lot of talking to do.

Chapter 28

Standing by the waffle maker in the hotel
lobby, Anna watched her family bustle around in
various areas of the room, piling their plates with
the smorgasbord. They were headed out shortly to
go visit the shops in town. Then, they planned to
surprise the boys with a trip to the go kart track.
Their father had told them to fill up before they left
because he was not feeding them again until lunch.
They were all doing very well at being obedient to
John's commands. Anna and Brooklyn were going
to go play skeet ball at the arcade next door and
play while the boys rode the cars.

Although the sun appeared brightly in the
sky today, the weather remained ambiguous. The
air was freezing, and if there was one thing Brooke
and Anna had in common, it was their dislike for
being cold. They all sat at a table for six that was
conveniently close to the biscuits and gravy table.
Blake informed them all that he would be headed
back there three more times at least before
breakfast was over. That kid would put gravy on
anything, and it made Anna smile as she wondered
where in the world he put it all.

Anna was happy to see that the whole family
was chipper and didn't show too many signs of the
stress of the past three months. Even Ben seemed

to be enjoying himself. Anna had been watching Ben, her middle child, very closely over the last couple of months. Ben really seemed to be going through some tough stuff these days, and his usually jovial, fun-loving self had been a little stifled, overshadowed by a bad attitude and argumentative spirit. Anna figured he had needed to get away as much as she did.

After clearing the tables, they all piled into the Expedition and headed to the shops. The kite shop was always a fave, and the boys left armed with rubber band guns and John, with a new stunt kite. In the game shop, Brooklyn found some fun brainteasers and Anna did her damage in the little soap shop. She loved the smell of the lemon essential oil soap, and every time she came to the beach she always ended up with a slice or two of the beautiful and aromatic delight.

The rest of the afternoon was filled with go karts, games, laughter, and ice cream. The evening was filled with board games by the fire in front of the picture window. Anna knew tomorrow would be full of more of the same. Now, Anna sat next to John. The kids were all tucked in bed watching Indiana Jones on the laptop in their little separate bedroom.

"Thanks again, John, for the most amazing Christmas gift."

"Well, I cannot lie. It was really not my idea. My mother had mentioned how stressed you've been lately. And Pastor Joe said you mentioned you needed a beach trip the other day. Then the final clincher was Jessica giving me a $200 Visa gift card and telling me to take Anna to the beach for Christmas. And, well, I may have had some help with my gift planning this year. I was gonna get you a vacuum cleaner."

Anna turned to John and jokingly slugged him in the arm. "Beach is always a better choice than a cleaning tool!"

"I will remember that," John said with a chuckle. The fire light was warm and the sky and ocean were dark. Anna was content right there in that moment. The songs of the old hymn began to play in Ann's mind: *peace like a river . . . when sorrows like sea billows roll.* Whatever came at her in this life time, Anna knew, no matter what, *it is well with my soul.* The Lord had taught her well, that in this world we will have trouble, but His word promised that she could take heart because God had overcome the world. And with that, Anna picked up her tea mug and her fuzzy blanket, put the mug into the sink, and headed towards the hotel bed, with John closely on her heals.

Jax had talked Collin into getting a couple hours of sleep on the couch before heading back to Belfair to see Delaney and Riley. Now it was 6:30 a.m. and he was sitting in the Jantzen Beach McDonald's drive through off of I-5. It had been a toss-up between here and the Starbucks on the other side of the highway, and Collin had decided on the less expensive option to end the music notes created by his stomach.

His GPS said he had 2 hours and 36 minutes before he arrived on Delaney's door step. Collin had never in his life wondered or worried about money. As a matter of fact, Collin had never even had a real job. Hid dad had always been quick to give him the cash he needed and to spoil him with gifts of anything he wanted. Wow, were things going to be different now. Collin had always spent the summers before his senior year going to work with his dad, watching him in action whenever he could. The more he thought about it, the more he realized he was fooling himself.

This last year, Collin had been sure his dad was pouring Carter Haggerty's dreams down

Collins throat when in fact, Collin suddenly remembered how he had developed the dreams of being a lawyer all on his own. No wonder his father had been so shocked when he threw his dream away to head to Northwest. His father did not understand this yearning Collin had in his heart to help others. Carter Haggerty was a business man, a hard nose with a killer instinct that he had sworn he saw in his son as well.

Collin was instantly aware of how confused he was feeling. Was he doing the right thing? Collin was sure he was going to marry Delaney at the end of this week, and he was more than ready to jump at being the father he needed to be. These things were obvious; the confusion came when Collin thought of his future occupation. Not that Collin wanted to be rich—that was not it at all. Was there a way to do law and satisfy his father, and *also* do ministry? Could the two very different worlds coexist?

Collin started driving again. Now in Centralia, he could not wait to get back to Belfair. He wanted to talk to Delaney; he wanted to make a plan. He wanted to create a dream.

Collin could not talk to Delaney right now, but he knew that he could actually talk to someone even better. And Collin spent the last hour of his

trip, after exiting onto Highway 101, praying for his
father, that God would help him find a way to reach
common ground.

Lacey and Cara bustled around their huge
home, collecting anything and everything they
might be needing over the next week. Carter
Haggerty sat at his giant mahogany desk, fighting
with everything inside of him to look strong. Last
night, as he fought for control, he explained to his
wife of 28 years that he would not stop her from
heading off to god-knows-where to help plan a
wedding that was sure to ruin her son's life. He
would not stop her, but he would most
definitely not come with her. Last night and this
morning, there was something very different about
Lacey. She seemed so calm, so peaceful. Carter was
sure she had been drinking again, yet it seemed a
bit different than her usual episodes. Carter hoped
she had not started taking something else. Drugs—
now that would be absolutely fantastic.

Their circle was large, but the affluent people
of Tualatin, Tigard, Lake Oswego, and the greater
Portland area, talked. It was shocking how fast a
story of a wife scorned or a drunken person making
a scene at an event could become today's latest and
greatest gossip. Lacey had always been so classy,

but over the last year, he had noticed her wine purchases becoming larger and less sporadic. And she had grown so distant. She rarely wanted to be intimate, and when she was, it seemed it was more out of duty than desire.

Lacey played her part well as a high society wife. Beautiful, charming, and sweet in public, at home she turned into a disconnected, cold, quiet wife. She needed to pull out of it or they were going to lose Cara, just as they were losing Collin. Maybe they already had.

Lacey came into the doorway of Carter's den and walked up behind her husband, putting her hand on his shoulder. He physically tensed under her touch. Lacey felt it, but she did not remove the offending hand.

"We are headed out now; we will be home on the third. I have written down all the information of where we are staying at the Alderbrook Resort & Spa. I have noted where and when the wedding will be as well. I do hope you change your mind, even though I do not expect that that will be the case. Cara and I will see you in a week. I have contacted Marta and let her know she would only be cooking for one this week, and she asked if she could make your meal ahead and leave it in the refrigerator so that she could come up to Washington and attend the big celebration. She said she would make sure the fridge is stocked with cold cuts and Figaro, from Cascade Brewery; she know it is your favorite and I think she is trying to cheer you up. Now, you could fend for yourself if you need to."

"I will be fine; please tell Marta thank you. I will not need her services at all while you guys are gone. She can consider it a paid vacation. I think I would like to be alone."

"Very well," Lacey said "we will all see you then in a week." Lacey felt awkward. She wanted to show her husband that she cared, but after over a year of little contact, and none of it having been instigated by her, Lacey felt strange. She just turned around and walked out of the ornate room her husband spent so much of his time in.

As he heard her footsteps fade, a cold chill fell over Carter. How had he ended up like this, so cold and alone? Hadn't he done everything he could to give everything possible to his wife and children? Now all he felt was betrayed. An hour ago, Carter had been sad; now, he was angry.

Carter stood up and exited the den where he felt like all he did these days was hide. The walls of his beloved den tonight felt more like prison walls. He had a whole house out there, and no one but himself to enjoy it with. Carter remembered his younger days when he and lacey used to have friends over to play bridge and canasta. They would laugh and joke, put back a few beers, and enjoy life. Where had those days gone? Those were the days before they had kids, before Collin and Cara. Carter had never been happier before that day when he brought his son to the office for the first time. Collin was eight years old. He could still picture the boy, spinning around in his chair. *I'm gonna be a lawyer just like you some day,* he had said. Had he just been telling his father what he wanted to hear? It sure had not felt like that. Carter felt certain that it was that girl. The day she left Collin, run away because she was knocked up, was the day his Collin had disappeared.

He could not show up at that wedding and put his stamp of approval on the worst decision his son would ever make. He would not give in. Carter loved his son, but he would not drive 200 miles to watch him throw his life away. One day, Collin would come crawling back to him and say he was sorry. Once the girl left him, because he could not provide for her, and once this God of his let him down one too many times, then he would run back. And only then would Carter take him back.

God? Where was this God when his dad was beating the life out of his mother? Where was God on the nights Carter's own father would drink himself into a stupor? That God was whom Collin had abandoned him for—God and a girl with a baby. Carter headed out to the theater room and put in a James Bond movie. Tonight, he would simply get lost in someone else's life. His own was just too much.

Chapter 29

Delaney had awoken early. Collin had texted her just after 6:00, saying that he had just left Portland. It was now 8:15. He should be here within the hour, bearing with the trouble of traffic due to the wintery weather. Delaney looked out the bay window of her beachside bedroom that looked over the South Shore waters. She sure would hate to leave this place once she and Collin got married at the end of the week. It was such an incredible way to wake up each morning. Delaney thought about how great it would be to wake up in this room with Collin by her side.

Delaney thought back to the months before she came to Belfair, when she was sleeping in her car or cheap hotel rooms. Delaney was really blessed. The scene outside was frosted and magical. The snow was falling in beautiful, fat flakes. They had about two inches of snow on the shore, and more fresh snow was forecasted to fall all day long. The sky, though gray, was beautifully serene. The view was like a picture you would see on a Christmas card. She could hardly wait for Collin to arrive. They had so much to talk about—not just the wedding plans, but the future. Delaney refused to freak out or panic. She had the strange feeling everything would come together.

In his texts last night, Collin had sounded like things went less than stellar with his father. Mr. Haggerty was a bit frightening to Delaney. He has harsh, controlling, and most of all, intimidating. Delaney knew that Collin loved his father, but it was honestly hard to imagine growing up under the scrutiny of such a man. It made Delaney very thankful for her own father. Franklin Evans had been all hugs and kisses with her in her younger years. He had encouraged her to dream, supported her endeavors, and funded her every whim. Delaney felt an overwhelming excitement that her parents were back in her life. How long had she planned to keep Riley from them? What was she thinking? She could have headed home the very day he had been born. Yet here she was, landed in Belfair.

Thank God her parents had pursued her and come searching. Who knows how long she would have let her pride keep her heart hidden? Delaney thought about that word *pursuit.* The more she thought about it, the more it seemed that that is was what was happening between her and God— that He had been pursuing her. It was so clear in her mind that God alone had brought Anna into her life at the hospital that night. And again, another God thing when she met Jessica Winters. Then there was this crazy town of Belfair, the whole student drama team at her church, and finally, her parents and Collin, all finding her right when she was ready for them. The more she thought about it, she realized that God had used her story, her mistake, and her shame to make her vulnerable to His love and pursuit.

On Christmas day, before Delaney left, Anna had told her that God worked all things for good for those who loved Him. Delaney did love God, and she was starting to feel like God Himself had landed her smack dab in the middle of this crazy situation. The moment she conceived little Riley, God had made a plan for intervention. God had made a way for redemption. The more time she spent reading the special Bible Jessica had given her for Christmas, and the more time she spent talking to God over these last two days, the more she knew that God had a plan for her and a plan for her son. And now, it seemed, a plan for her first love as well. Delaney could not wait to see what that plan was.

Collin was getting closer. He had entered Shelton, and the roads were pretty bad. It was making his trip longer, and he could hardly wait to see his wife-to-be. Seventeen miles per hour! This was crazy. He wanted to make it there in one piece, however, so slow and steady he went. He was blaring Rascal Flatts on his Bose speakers, singing about regrets and moving on. Collin thought about how he had once regretted the mistakes he made with Delaney, and as much as he wished it hadn't happened quite like this, his regret was exchanged for anticipation of the future. He was still trying to wrap his head around the fact that Delaney was back in his life. He was flabbergasted by the reality that he was also a father. Collin thought of his own dad back home. That was his biggest regret. He regretted that he could not reach his father, and he regretted that his father saw God as the problem and not the solution in his life. Collin knew there was very little chance that his father would show up in Belfair on New Year's, but Collin was not worried about that. Carter Haggerty was a stubborn man. Collin was much more worried about the possibility that his father would never give his heart to Jesus. Collin pulled off Highway 3 and onto Highway 106. He was close, now. In another five minutes or so, Delaney would be in his arms and he would get to hold that beautiful boy of his. For the last few minutes of the drive, Collin prayed for his father. He prayed for his salvation, and he prayed for a line of protection to be drawn around him, until that day of salvation came.

Lacey and Cara decided to get an early start that morning. It would take about three and a half hours to get to the Alderbrook, and they planned to stop at the mall for some baby and wedding gifts on the way. And the way Lacey loved to shop, it could take a little time. So at about 8:15, she and Cara headed out the door. Lacey pulled a small note out of her purse that she had written for Carter the night before and placed it on his night stand. Carter was under a lot of stress right now, and she knew he needed sleep. She was sure he had probably popped a couple of Tylenol PMs last night, so he might be out of commission for a while. She leaned down, kissed her husband on the cheek, and headed out the door with Cara right behind her.

Carter woke up Friday morning to an empty house. It was a little before 9:00, and Carter could think of absolutely nothing to do. Knowing Collin was coming home, he had impulsively taken a few extra days off of work—poor planning on his part. Little did he know that he would now be spending three days home alone. This simply would not do. Carter would precipitately find an excuse to head into the office. Most of his colleagues were off for the week for the holiday, but he was sure he would find one or two workaholics there, no matter what the season. He felt sad for himself that he was among those few. Suddenly, Carter remembered his threat to Collin. Carter walked to his den, picked up the phone, and promptly canceled Collin's credit card. Then, he pulled up his and Collin's joint checking account online and transferred all but $500 dollars out of it. After a quick shower and a power bar, Carter felt pretty good about himself and headed to the office.

After pulling into the parking lot of Ames, Haggerty, & Jones, a heaviness fell over Carter. It was accompanied by a bitterness that clung to him like a dying man clinging to life. He exited his BMW M3 and walked the few feet to the back entrance. The lot was virtually empty, save a handful of cars. It was nearing 10:00 a.m., so anyone who was coming in for the day was already here. Carter stuck his key into the lock and pulled open the doors. As the warm air hit him, he felt as if he were coming home. This was the place where he was at his best, the place he was appreciated. This place was where he made a difference. He was respected when he was inside these walls—honored, even. A small twinge of guilt settled in his mind for a mere moment, but Carter pushed it away almost as quickly as it came. He was not driving to Belfair. Not tonight, tomorrow, or anytime. He was going to go to work and put all thought of marriage and grandchildren and betrayal away from him.

Jenna Jones was standing at the copier, waiting for some papers to finish printing, when Carter walked by. "I hate this ridiculous machine," Jenna said to Carter as he passed. "We spend thousands of dollars a month to keep up the best equipment, and it still jams."

Carter walked into the copy room to see if he could help. Jenna and Carter had been working together for about four years now, since her father Marcus had suddenly passed away of a heart attack. Jenna had taken his place as a partner. She graduated from Princeton at the top of her class five years ago, and at 28, she was one of the toughest go-getter lawyers the firm had. She was smart and vivacious. It was almost as if she had something to prove to her father, like he was still pushing her to be better and fight harder, even from the grave.

"Here, let me take a look at it," Carter said. Jenna looked up at Carter with big eyes.

"Thanks so much, Carter, that would be great."

Carter bent down on the side of the machine and opened Door C, where the miss-feed was allegedly lodged, and saw nothing.

"I looked there, too," Jenna said, leaning in close to Carter. Her body brushed against him, shocking Carter with the sudden sensation of electricity. Carter reached further into the machine and lifted a toggle attached to a roller inside the printer. He fished out a piece of torn paper.

"It really was in there! Wow, thanks!" Jenna said. "I have been fighting with this stupid machine for fifteen minutes trying to figure out its malfunction. Then you, in thirty seconds, swoop in like Superman and save the day." Jenna gave Carter her biggest smile, showing off plump red lips and her white teeth. Carter could remember those teeth in braces. He needed to pull himself together. Jenna was born the year he got married! He was married, he suddenly reminded himself. Not to mention that he was twenty-four years Jenna's senior and had gone to law school with Jenna's father.

What was he doing, thinking about how good she looked? Carter was suddenly overwhelmed by Jenna's perfume and this copy room seemed very small. He closed the side panel door on the copier and started to back out of the cramped quarters. He was having a hard time taking his eyes off of Jenna, who was wearing a tight-fitted V-neck tee and tight yoga pants on her relaxed day in the office. For a second, he found himself looking down at Jenna's cleavage, allowing him mind to travel, and he had to force himself to turn around. He headed to his office and closed the door, hoping Jenna had not noticed how he was ogling her, how his body was betraying him by reacting to her closeness. Carter sat down at his desk overlooking the city of Portland and took a few slow breaths. So, maybe his office wasn't the place to come if he wanted peace. But he sure had loved the way she called him Superman. Carter poured himself a scotch and downed it fast, and then he poured another. After his third quick hit, Carter was beginning to feel calmer. He was instantly sure that his attraction for Jenna was one-sided. He was over fifty years old; surely Jenna Jones was completely unaware of his longing libido.

What was that? Jenna thought, as she walked out of the copy room with her freshly printed papers in hand. Since when did she flirt with the men of the office? Jenna had always looked up to and admired Carter Haggerty, and with his Richard Gere looks, there was most definitely nothing unattractive about the older man. But he was married, happily or not, and that made him forbidden fruit. You simply did not touch the untouchable. That would not only be playing with fire, but also a possible career-ender. But dang, there was definitely chemistry there. Jenna had always found him attractive, always noticed him when he walked into a room, but this was the first time she had ever detected him noticing her back.

Jenna went back to her office and sat in her chair. How funny that he would notice her with barely any makeup on, and in her workout gear. Men were so unpredictable, yet so predictable at the same time. As if she were being taken over by the invasion of the body snatchers, Jenna began to devise a plan of how she could meet up with Carter Haggerty again today. She wasn't going to actually do anything; she just wanted to see if it happened again, that feeling, or if it had just been in her imagination. That was all—she just needed to see. And after all, he was here when he was scheduled to be off on vacation with his family, so maybe he needed to talk, or needed help with some work, so he could get things done a little faster. Now her mind was going, and Jenna suddenly needed to be near Carter. Just to see what would happen.

Chapter 30

Collin finally arrived at Delaney's house just after 11:00. It was much later than he had planned, but after getting breakfast, grabbing a bouquet of flowers for Delaney, and the inclement road conditions, he was way off schedule. When she opened the door, she was a sight for sore eyes. Delaney welcomed Collin in.

"I am just getting ready to feed Riley, but you can come on in." Collin handed Delaney the bouquet of roses and Delaney's face lit up. "Oh, Collin, they are beautiful. Here—take him and I will put them in some water." She handed Riley over to Collin and the little guy went with no fuss at all.

"I also brought brownies," Collin said.

"Marta's brownies?" Delaney squealed.

"Yes, Marta's brownies."

"Awesome! I get super hungry when I am nursing." Suddenly Delaney looked awkward, but no more so than Collin felt. Her cheeks were blushing, but Collin was sure his were as well. Delaney grabbed the brownies out of his hands, all four of them, then grabbed Riley and ran up the stairs. Collin had been planning to eat at least one of those brownies, but decided to call them a loss to the nursing mom. It was all still so surreal.

Collin sat down on the sofa and stared out the window. While he had been off to school pretending to be an adult, Delaney was delivering a baby, tending to his sickness, making plans for survival, and learning how to take care of, nurse, and nurture a kid. His entire last year suddenly seemed frivolous and wasted. He should have been helping her, but instead she had had to do it all on her own! He was about to marry the strongest women he had ever met. He might be the luckiest man alive. No, not lucky, but blessed, Collin Haggerty was blessed.

Jenna thought long and hard about how she was going to orchestrate a chance meeting with Carter again, and she came up with nothing. Then she heard the door to his office open. She suddenly remembered—coffee! Carter drank coffee. She saw Carter step into the restroom and she slipped out into the coffee lounge. She scooped what she hoped was the right amount of coffee grounds into the pot and hit the brew button. Jenna was not a coffee drinker, but she had made coffee for the firm for six months before her father started accepting that she was actually a lawyer. She had watched many a pot made since. There was no way Carter paid enough attention over the years to realize she was a green tea girl.

She heard footsteps coming down the hall and she felt her heart rate quicken. What was she, sixteen again and crushing on a teacher? *Seriously*, Jenna thought, *grow up.* Jenna's hands were a bit wobbly and just then, Jenna dropped the mug she was holding precisely as Carter rounded the corner. Jenna quickly bent over to pick up the broken shards of ceramic from the tile floor, pretending she had not noticed Carter walk in the room.

Carter stood in the doorway, staring dumbly as Jenna bent over in her skin-tight yoga pants. What was she doing to him, trying to drive him crazy? He noticed every curve of her body. He wanted to be closer to this mesmerizing enchantress. It was as if she had cast a spell on him. He was out of his mind and the scotch was not helping him think clearly.

He walked over to Jenna and touched the small of her back. "You are a very beautiful woman, Jenna," he said in a low voice.

Jenna stayed bent over the broken fragments. "I am very attracted to you as well," she answered seductively. She slowly rose from her task of cleaning. They stood there frozen like that for a moment, Carter contemplating what to do next.

As Marta popped over to the Haggerty house to drop off the groceries, she had the most overwhelming sense come over her. Carter was not home; he must have gone to work. But Marta suddenly had the feeling that she needed to pray. And then, right there in the Haggerty's kitchen, Marta knelt on the floor and began to intercede for the Haggerty family, but especially for the senior Mr. Haggerty.

Like a glass of cold water in the face, Carter heard the closing of a door. Jenna heard it as well, and turned her body away from the doorway facing Carter. With the pieces of mug still in her hand, she stepped away from his closeness toward the trash can. Lois Cranson, one of the office secretaries who had been working at the firm for over twenty years, came past the lounge and offered her greeting to the two lawyers. Giving a quick greeting in return, Carter turned around, left the lounge, and headed back to his office.

Jenna was mortified. What had just happened? What *would* have just happened if Lois had not come in? Jenna quickly scrolled a note to Carter on a napkin.

Mr. Haggerty,

I am sorry if I acted inappropriately. I am not sure what came over me—the loneliness of the holiday, I suppose. I am headed home now, and I suppose you should do the same. Your wife I am sure would love to have you home during this holiday. She is a very nice lady.

Merry Christmas, Mr. Haggerty.

Jenna

She took the note and slipped it under Carter's door before she had a chance to think more about it. Then Jenna went home.

In his office, Carter sat down at his chair, put his head into his hands, and began to weep. What had he just done? Carter might have hated the things happening in his life right now, but he was not a cheater. How could he have been entertaining the thought he was entertaining? Thank goodness for Lois. Carter noticed a napkin sliding under his door. He stood up and quickly retrieved it. He read the note and then tossed it into his gas fireplace and watched it burn. The smell of it burning was a clear reminder of the stupid thing he had almost done.

Collin stood to his feet and walked out his office door, turning off the fireplace and his light. As he passed the lounge, he smelled the coffee Jenna made. He had full knowledge that Jenna was a tea drinker. Carter hit the off switch on the pot and was about to dump the coffee into the sink when he heard footsteps behind him. He turned to see Lois Cranson standing in the doorway.

"I sure hope I didn't interrupt anything earlier," she said with a knowing look in her eye.

"Oh no, of course not. I was getting ready to call it an afternoon anyway," Carter said, feeling the need to explain himself to this woman even though she had no business being nosy.

"Oh good, good, then," Lois said. "I just had the strangest feeling I left the fireplace on in the main lobby and I wouldn't have wanted to be responsible for burning the place down, now would I?"

"Of course not, Ms. Cranson" Carter said with a half smile. *We were the ones needing our flames put out,* he thought.

"I hope you have a very happy New Year's, Mr. Haggerty. And please tell Lacey I said happy New Year's as well," Lois said with what seemed like a knowing smile. Carter at that moment was not sure if the universe was looking out for him or messing with him, but either way, he was heading home where it was safe.

When Carter arrived home, Marta's car was in the driveway.

"Hello," Carter said as he came into the kitchen. Marta looked up from the chair she was kneeling in front of.

"Oh, Mr. Carter sir, are you all right?" she said. "I had the heaviest burden to pray for you, like something horrible was about to happen."

Carter walked over to the older woman, giving her a hand as she stood. "How long have you been praying here, Marta?" Carter asked, noticing the tearstain trail down the woman's cheeks.

"Oh, an hour or so," Marta replied. "When it is time to do the Lord's business, you get on your knees and you don't get up until the business is done."

Carter had the strangest feeling as Marta spoke. "Well, Marta, maybe you saved me from a car accident, or a train wreck," he said, knowing it was a train wreck he had avoided for sure.

"Yes, maybe so," Marta said. "But it was not me who saved you, Mr. Carter. It was the Lord who put you in my heart to pray. So you can thank Him, Mr. Carter. I will be on my way now, now I know you are all safe and sound. Good night, Mr. Carter. Hope you figure out everything you need to figure out and that you find what you are searching for."

Carter walked to his study and just stood there. What in the world had just happened? Marta, his cook and house keeper, on her knees crying and praying for him? And Lois—that timing seemed just a little too perfect. Carter could be living with some serious regret right now. Did he really have an old Italian lady to thank for preventing him from jumping in the sack with his 28-year-old colleague? Life made absolutely no sense to Carter right now.

It was only 4:00, but Carter Haggerty was weary to the bone and he was going to bed. Popping two Tylenol PMs into his mouth, Carter put on his pajama pants and climbed into his king-sized bed. Before he knew it, he was out.

Chapter 31

Anna put on her warm winter coat and got ready to head to the beach for one last walk before they had to leave the next morning. It had been wonderful to get away, but Anna was ready to get back and help with the last minute plans for the wedding. Ben came into the room and she was getting ready to head out.

"Want some company?" He said to his mom.

"You know I do," Anna said, "go grab your jacket. It is freezing out there!" Anna had been waiting for this opportunity to get Ben alone and check on him. He had not been himself lately.

As they walked on the beach, the wind started to pick up. Anna knew they wouldn't be able to tolerate the cold long, so she got right to it.

"So how are you doing these days, Ben?"

"Not so great, I guess."

"What's up, kiddo? I have notice you are really bothered by something."

"Yeah, I guess I am." They walked a few more feet in silence. It appeared that Ben needed a minute to get his thoughts together.

"I am struggling, Mom."

"What are you struggling with, Ben?"

"Well," Ben said, "I guess I am struggling with church." Anna reached over and put her hand on Ben's shoulder.

"What about church?" She asked.

"Well," Ben thought for a second, "I know God is real and I know Jesus loves me—I am not questioning that—but sometimes I get frustrated with church. I get frustrated with people who say they are Christians and then don't act like it. I am sick and tired of people who are so judgmental and unkind about things that other people are struggling with. And I get angry when you seem to give all of your time to the church instead of us."

Anna stopped in the sand and pulled Ben's hand, turning him towards her. When had he become so tall, and so grown up, and so wise?

"Well Ben, herein lies the dilemma: first, the church would be perfect without imperfect people. Yet, it is all of us and our imperfect ways that create a need for God. You are right—some so-called Christians are jerks. Some lack compassion and some lack kindness. But we have to worry about the fruit of the Spirit that is evident in our own lives.

The fruit of the Spirit is love, joy, peace, patience, kindness, goodness, faithfulness, gentleness, and self-control. We cannot regulate these virtues in the lives of others, but we *can* make sure that they are evident in our own lives. In fact, the Lord wants us to make sure they are.

"As for people being judgmental, I hear you there, too. I am reminded of the scripture—I think it is in Matthew—that says, "He who is without sin, cast the first stone." There was a woman who had been caught cheating on her husband, and the penalty for that at the time was death by stoning. As this woman stood there, with ripped clothes and a broken heart, Jesus drew a line in the sand! I can just imagine it. You see, the Pharisees, the religious leaders of the time, had a bit of a dilemma. They had decided this woman was wrong and they were judging her according to her sin, and Jesus told them, go ahead! If *you* have never sinned, throw the rocks—kill the woman. If the leaders picked up a stone, they were saying they were perfect; and if they didn't, they were saying they were sinners and classifying themselves with the common sinners. They did not know what to do, but in that moment, they decided to show fake mercy. Jesus then turned to the woman and told her to go and to sin no more. We live in a world where people seem to throw stones at one another without thought of whether or not they are guilty of sinning themselves. And, once again, I have only one solution for you. Watch yourself. Keep yourself accountable to make sure you are not being the one to cast the judgment.

"As for my taking more time for others than for you, I am sorry. I am going to make a genuine effort to make sure I am here for you, so we can talk and keep on the same page. I love you so much, Ben. I want to be there for you. I am sorry I have failed in that way!"

Ben reached over and hugged his mom. "Thanks, Mom, I feel a little better now. Thanks for taking a walk with me. And I love you, too." Anna's heart felt full at that moment. How she loved this boy. Anna knew that she needed to make sure she made her kids her priority. It had always been her goal, and right now, she was making plans in her head of different ways she could connect on a deeper level with each of her children. They meant the world to her and she was for sure going to make sure they knew how much they were loved.

Saturday morning, Carter woke with a headache that rivaled all others. His head was pounding. He walked into his den and opened his top desk drawer, retrieving a small bottle of pain killers he kept in there. He took three into his hand and walked into the kitchen. Opening the fridge, he looked at the water bottles on the shelf, and then instead he pulled out a Figaro from the top shelf. He twisted the wire *muselet* cage from around the cork. Once again, he said a silent thanks to Marta. With the beer, he threw back the three pills in his hand and attempted to figure out what he was going to do with himself today.

With no ability to think beyond the happenings of yesterday, Carter walked back into the den. Sitting at his desk, he thought about how lost he felt. He couldn't go into the office, that was certain. He couldn't go to Belfair where his family was, and he for sure did not want to stay here in this house all alone. It was 10:17. The grandfather clock in the corner of the room seemed to sneer at him with a promise to move its hands as slowly as possible.

Just then, the phone rang. He fumbled with the noisy device.

"Hello?" He answered.

"Hello, Carter." He heard his wife's voice on the other line, and guilt flooded him, threatening to drown him. Not wanting to sound suspicious, and not wanting to talk about himself, Carter asked

Lacey how her and Cara's trip had been. Lacey filled him in on the details, and told him about his first grandson. She told him how the boy had been very sick, having congenital heart failure. How he had had surgery to fix the problem. How he had blue eyes and blond curls like Collin. Lacey did not beg him to come to the wedding, or try to make him feel guilty. She just told him that she loved him and that she was praying for him. She also apologized for being insensitive to the fact that this had all hurt his feelings. Carter felt like she was heaping hot coals upon his head with her kindness. Finally, before she hung up, her last words were, "God loves you, Carter. We will make it through this. At least we still have each other." Robotically, Carter told his wife that he loved her too and hung up the phone.

What was going on here? Carter was overwhelmed. He returned to his room, put his head on his pillow, and hoped he could just fall asleep.

Lacey, Cara, and Dolores all drove together to meet Delaney in Silverdale. Delaney and Collin had been out and about since 9:00 that morning, finishing up the last details. Friday, they had gone together and gotten their marriage license. Today had been all about going to Bainbridge Island to the

Blackbird Bakery, where Delaney had found the most perfect three-tiered cake, all white, with the most beautiful sugar snowflakes embossed on it. The three other ladies were all excitedly chattering away about how in the world this could all be happening. Collin was going to drop off Delaney at The Habit, where they would all grab lunch before heading to Benita's Bridal to get fitted for their dresses. Everything was going to be extra costly because of the short notice and crazy rush on everything. Thanks, however, to Franklin's credit card, cost was no object.

Sitting inside the restaurant waiting for Delaney to show up, Lacey told Dolores how amazing it was that she and Franklin had found Delaney again.

"When Collin came home and said he had found her, and that you had been reunited with her as well, I could only think, 'wow, miracles do happen.' And a Christmas miracle, at that!"

Cara seemed to look a little uncomfortable with this sudden God talk coming from her mother. Something had changed with Cara's mother this week. Cara could not pinpoint exactly what it was, but she both liked the change and was scared of it at the same time. As a Catholic school girl, Cara had been filled with notions and ideas about God since the first grade. Yes, there were just enough nuns that were forward thinking about women's rights that she could tuck all of the God stuff in its place, and out of her mind. So all of a sudden, her mother joining the religious bandwagon was a little too much. Over the years, Cara had noticed that just like some people looked to the stars for guidance, others depended on an invisible God. Whatever they needed to be their crutch was fine, as long as they didn't push it off on her. Cara didn't need anything or anyone. Trusting people was a great thought until they decided to step out on you.

Dolores spoke up after Lacey's comment about the Christmas miracle. "I had nearly given up hope that Delaney was okay. As a mom, I wondered if she would ever come home safe and sound. When Delaney left, she took a piece of my heart with her. I have experienced just about every negative emotion you could imagine this last year and a half. I have been sad, angry, bitter, depressed, anxious, and afraid. I had only a slim bit of hope left. I feared I would find her shacked up with some guy, strung out on drugs, or homeless on the streets, at best. You can't even know how relived I was to find out she had been living in a beautiful home with a waterfront view, working as a housekeeper and spending every extra hour she had with a children's pastor, playing the piano for a kids' musical theater group. It was like, in one moment, all of my fears were replaced with the strangest feeling of joy and relief mixed together. I am not going to lie—I was also a little bit angry until I saw a better picture of the circumstances."

"Riley," Lacey said.

"Yes, Riley was the beginning of it, and then I realized Delaney's fears of what would happen to her baby if she had stayed home." Cara actually got where Dolores was coming from in her anger at Delaney for leaving, but that didn't excuse Delaney's behavior just because she was pregnant. Lacey, on the other hand, gave Dolores a knowing look. She had no clue about the journals, or the fact that Dolores had herself aborted a baby, but she knew exactly what Carter Haggerty would have wanted done. He would have seen it as the only way to save the future of his only son.

"Anyway, it is all so unbelievable, what is happening here," Dolores said, "and Lacey, I think perhaps you are right—God may just have something to do with it."

At that moment, Delaney walked into the burger place and waved at the three ladies sitting in the booth. Cara scooted over to make room for her and all talk of the past ten minutes was put away.

Cara's mind, however, was still working things out. She was trying to be cordial, yet inside was wondering what to do with the feelings of hurt the young woman beside her had left in her destructive wake when she skipped town all those months ago.

"So now, who has little Riley today while we are out?" Lacey asked Delaney.

"Well, believe it or not, he is hanging out with my dad and Collin is on his way to join them for a boys' day. They are hanging out at Jessica's while we have our girls' day. I just can't believe it. Riley just loves Collin and my dad, too. It is like he knows somehow that they are family."

"That is great," Dolores said.

"It is so good. I was a little nervous about it, since he has not been around many men. Other than John James, whom he loves to pieces, and our pastor, he is mostly around girls. Although, he has really taken a liking to Ben and Blake, Anna James' sons, but then again, what's not to like? Those boys are a bundle of fun."

"I ordered the teriyaki burger for you," Dolores told her daughter, "and some onion rings."

"Awesome, thanks Mom." It felt so good to say that word *Mom*. They ate their burgers, and

Cara ate her vegan veggie burger, and then they were on their way.

The fittings went well. Jessica had agreed to meet them at the store to get her dress fit. The dresses were all so beautiful. Cara had agreed to be a bridesmaid, and Jessica was to be the matron of honor. The deep red satin dresses were stunning in the way they fit each of the slender bridesmaids. Cara had only agreed to play the role because she was pretty sure that Jax was coming up to be in the wedding, and Cara hoped they would be partnered together. Collin had also asked John James to be a groomsman. The two men, although they had not known each other long, had formed a quick bond united by their common love for dirt bikes, Mustangs, and Jesus. They were a match made in heaven, Anna had told them.

Lacey walked over to the tuxedo area of the bridal shop and fingered the cuff of a sleeve on a mannequin. *Lord, be with Carter today and somehow get ahold of his heart.* She knew there was very little chance that her husband would come to the wedding, which was just a few short days away. She touched the fabric, however, and imagined her husband in the suit and bow tie, cummerbund in place, seated next to her as their only son took a crazy step into marriage. Carter would not have it.

Arriving at that wedding on Tuesday would be stamping his approval on immature love. And she knew the chances of hell freezing over were greater than Carter showing up.

Carter went to the fridge, grabbed another beer, twisted the cage, and popped the cork as he walked, letting it fall to the ground. It was 3:30 p.m. and now the last of the beers were gone. What was he doing? Carter was beginning to think that maybe things would just be easier if he got in his BMW and drove to Washington.

He drained the last sip out of the beer bottle and walked over to his liquor cabinet. He took out an old bottle of single malt bourbon and began to pour a glass. He downed it fast, and then he downed another. Carter was starting to feel a little more relaxed; yet, he was also feeling agitated. Maybe he would do it—head to Washington and give these kids a piece of his mind. Married at nineteen? What were they thinking?

Carter walked over to the table, grabbed his keys, then turned to the coat rack to grab his coat. He walked out to the first garage where his car was parked. He started the car and pulled out onto the circular drive. Carter made his way into town and then finally, he pulled onto I-405. That's when he saw the flashing lights pull up behind him. And for the first time in many years, Carter Haggerty was afraid.

Carter pulled his car over to the side of the road. The officer came up to Carter's window after what seemed like forever. A cold blast of sobering air hit Carter in the face as he rolled down the car window.

"Excuse me, sir," the officer said, "have you been drinking?" Carter did not answer. "Sir, I am going to ask you to get out of your vehicle." Carter opened the door of his car and got to his feet. He stumbled a bit and then felt as though he was standing still against the frame of his car.

"Sir, I have reason to believe that you are under the influence of some substance." The young officer could, without a doubt, smell the alcohol on Carter's breath. "I am going to administer a breathalyzer test, sir. Please stay right here with your hand placed firmly on your car." The fear Carter had been feeling a moment ago was replaced with terror. Suddenly, Carter knew that he was going to jail and there was nothing he could do about it. Carter thought for a moment about the law and about applied consent. In Oregon, he had the right to refuse to take the test. For a moment,

Carter thought about the fact that he could refuse. But it was without a doubt that he was stone cold drunk, and refusal to blow the test would probably backfire on him. So he blew a 0.21 BAC. Before he knew it, Carter heard the words, "You are under arrest. You have the right to remain silent, and you have the right to an attorney." An attorney? Carter was an attorney. This was completely unreal.

Carter was cuffed and put into the back of a squad car, and as if things couldn't get any worse, he was sure he had recognized at least three people he knew driving by. The cold air and humiliation had sobered Carter just a little, and he was sure someone should just kill him now.

The car smelled of stale sweat and vomit, probably from some deadbeat picked up before him. This was not right; he did not belong here.

Upon arrival at the jail, Carter was asked if he had anyone he wanted to call. It was like having a nightmare where he was an actor in a low budget cop show. But the reality was, Carter had no one. Although he was sure this was ludicrous and ill-advised, Carter gave the officer the number of Jenna Jones. Carter was then escorted to a large holding cell, where his cuffs were taken off and the door was slammed behind him. The cell smelled of old urine and Carter was unsure where to sit. He could hear the harsh cursing of the man sitting towards the back of the cell. There was a young kid, maybe eighteen, just about Collins age, sporting a black eye and a huge fat lip. There was also a massive African American man, twice Carter's size, yet he had a lost, sad look in his eyes. There was the cursing man in the back who looked half-crazed, half-baked, and homeless. Lastly, there was a tall guy with dreadlocks and baggy cargo pants. He had colorful embroidery floss woven into his dreads that matched his poncho, and Birkenstocks tied the outfit together, worn with thick woolen socks.

For a moment, Carter began to think about what had brought each of these men to the place they were in. Why were they here? Carter knew full well that, as the man who had never been anywhere but on the other side of these bars, he was the poster boy for a judgmental white collar jerk. Yet here, sitting in this holding room waiting to be booked, Carter Haggerty felt very humble. Each of these men had a story. Each of them brought here, accused of a crime under some sort of specific circumstances.

Suddenly, Carter stepped over to the small thing resembling a toilet and puked his guts out. *Dear God, how did I get here?* Carter thought to himself. What in the world had he done, and how in the heck was he going to get out of it? Hopelessness shrouded him like a heavy blanket that he was not strong enough to remove.

Carter had sworn he would never become his father. He had promised himself that remaining in control of life was only possible if he stayed sober. He had even chastised his wife for her nightly glass of wine. He saved any kind of drinking to be done at minimum. Carter had relied on his abundant strength to keep him on the straight and narrow. He didn't cheat on his wife, he didn't drink in excess, he supported his kids, and he didn't commit crimes. And then, in one twenty-four hour period, he had committed the sins of his father—all of them.

Carter had spent years convincing Lacey that there was no god she could trust. The Catholic schools were just an image people painted and used to keep up with the Joneses. What if the God that he had all but forced Lacey to give up, was real? What if he was wrong? What if there *was* a God, and what if this God was trying to teach him something?

By 2:00 a.m. on Sunday morning, Officer Jamison Cross was nearly ready to process one Carter Haggerty. Jamison had been called in for an extra shift tonight; apparently Portland was alive and well with crime. Jamison had accepted the extra hours, knowing that his little family could really use the money. His little girl had been struggling after her life-saving surgery three weeks ago. The bills had not yet started to roll in, but he knew they would soon.

Jamison grabbed his clipboard and looked at the bio he had on Carter. Caucasian male, age 53, lawyer at Ames, Haggerty, & Jones. Address, Tualatin Valley Highlands. Weariness overcame Jamison. The very last thing he wanted to deal with tonight was a privileged white dude who was used to being on the other side of the law. Growing up in the projects of Gresham, Jamison had seen his share of struggles, his share of poverty, and for sure more than his share of crime. His own mother had frequented the justice system again and again. Venessa Cross could not say no to the feeling of crack in her system. Jamison's *oma* had taken his brother, sister, and himself in when Jamison was seven, his brother was five, and his sister was only two and a half. His mother's mother had seen it as the only option to keep the children off the street.

Jamison had become the sole caretaker of the two smaller children by the time he was five. He could remember the months before he moved in with his grandmother, walking his brother and sister to the park not far from their apartment. He remembered the street missionaries that came and made balloon animals and sang songs with them. Peanut butter and Jesus, they called themselves. Jamison remembered getting a jar of peanut butter and a loaf of white bread from them every time they came out to entertain the kids that summer. Jamison made sure every week they were there that he went with his siblings, and every time, each one of them left with the food that would sustain them for the week to come. Sometimes they would fix hot dogs at the park; sometimes they had sandwiches made for the kids, and then brought the sandwich makings to go. Every week on Friday afternoon they would show up, and every week Jamison would get his siblings there. After about five weeks, Jamison became comfortable with these teens and Pastor Tyrone, or P.T., as he was called. One day, P.T. asked Jamison if he could pray for him about anything. Jamison remembered how carful he had been not to mention his mom was a user. He had just said, "Well, I would pray that God will help me take care of my brother and sister." And Pastor Tyrone and several other teens prayed for him right there. Two weeks later, on August 12, 1997, his *oma* showed up at his door and Vanessa Cross handed her three children over to her mother without a question. From then on, times were tough for sure, but that year Jamison's *oma* took him to church. Jamison gave his life to Jesus. Vanessa Jamison went to jail time and time again, but Jamison learned what family was all about. There were no new men each week to beat the crap out of him, there were warm meals on the table each night, and he could go to school every day. Jamison was fifteen years old when he sat down with his *oma* after a speech by Nelson Mandela. His grandmother quoted to him these words: "As long as poverty, injustice, and gross inequality persist in our world, none of us can truly rest." She had continued, "We gotta pray, boy. You need to keep your nose clean, love on Jesus, stay away from the stuff that's gonna git you in trouble. You gotta look out for your little brother and help him see the way, and you need to take care of your sister. You gotta good head on your shoulders, Jamison. You keep your eyes on Jesus." It was during that conversation that Jamison decided to be a cop. He wanted to be a good cop who helped the kids in the hood stay out of trouble. And that is what he did. He worked hard and became a cop. It wasn't without ridicule. The insults were hurled like arrows at him in the beginning. But after five years on the Portland Police Department, he was finally gaining some respect as one of the good guys. Affluent white men, privileged and above the law, made him crazy. He was going to show this guy. Jamison Cross didn't show favoritism to the entitled.

Carter sat on the hard, cold bench, pondering his life. He wondered what the rest of his family was doing right now. Planning a wedding? Holding his grandson? Carter felt his eyes well up and suddenly remembered that he was in hostile territory. This would not be the place to show weakness. At that moment there in the room, Carter knew he had changes to make. Right there, his situation bleak, Carter closed his eyes and prayed to the God that seemed to be the One pulling the strings in his life.

Jamison rounded the corner to the holding cell. He walked with determined purpose. Glancing into the cell, it was not hard at all to spot Carter Haggerty. Jamison did not see what he expected to see. The rich man on that bench looked haggard, broken, tearful, and it seem as though he was in prayer.

Dear God, are you there? Carter prayed. *If you are, I need you now. I need your help. I need you to get me out of this. God, if you help me fix this and somehow come out of it without losing my job and my family, I just might give you a chance. I will go to church.* One single tear slid down Carter's face.

Jamison unlocked the cell door and called out Carter's name. Indeed, the man who stood up was exactly the one whom Jamison had expected, yet as much as Jamison had set out to be the lesson teacher this morning, instead he felt compassion. It seemed strange and misplaced, but undeniably, it was there. Carter rose to his feet and walked toward Officer Cross. He explained he would need to turn around and the cuffs would be put on again as he took him to booking.

"Yes sir," Carter said, and Jamison was sure he heard respect in Mr. Haggerty's voice. *How curious*, Jamison thought. *But for the grace of God, this could be you.* Jamison was sure he heard the still small voice of God, and he felt consumed by grace. Jamison led Carter through the steps and then informed him that his lawyer was waiting for him in a room around the corner. Carter looked up at the tall, young African American officer.

"Thank you, young man."

Jamison was not sure what God wanted from him at this point, so he just said, "Thank you. I will take you into the room where you can talk with your lawyer."

Carter looked again at Jamison, and said, "Can I ask you a question?"

"Yes sir, of course you can," Jamison answered.

"Are you a praying man?"

"Yes, I am."

"Well then, son, will you please pray for me? My life is in a bit of a bad place right now, and well, if there is really a God and He really cares anything about me, I really think I need His help."

Jamison answered with conviction in his voice. "Well, sir, as for there being a God that cares for you, I am completely convinced the answer is yes. The part where you asked me to pray, sir, I would tell you I already have been."

"Do you go to church, son?"

"Yes I do, sir. I attend Trinity Full Gospel Pentecostal Church."

"Well, maybe if I manage to clear this hurdle, I'll have to come and visit you there sometime."

Jamison smiled at the thought of this stiff old guy breaking it loose for Jesus with his people. "Well sir, I sure hope you do. Now let's go see what your lawyer can do for you!" Carter turned and headed towards the door, not letting his new ally-of-sorts see his discomfort at seeing Jenna.

Jenna Jones was in a conference room waiting for Carter Haggerty to enter. What in the heck had happened? Carter barely even drank. Of all of the partners in the office, Carter was the least likely to end up with a DUI. She had a very strong feeling his episode of sudden drunken stupidity had a lot to do with her.

The door opened and Jenna greeted Carter, who was accompanied by a tall officer who unlocked Carter's cuffs and led him into the room.

"I will be right outside, let me know when you are done," said Officer Cross.

"Thanks, Officer, and thanks for everything." Jenna was a little puzzled at the friendly way Carter spoke to the officer, but he had just spent the night in a jail cell, and she figured that could either harden or soften a man to the officers in authority over him.

Carter took a seat at the small Formica table in front of Jenna. "I am so sorry for everything," Carter said. "Then on top of it all, I had no idea who to call. First, I wanted to say I had no right to act the way I did Friday morning. I was disrespectful to you as a fellow partner; not to mention I am married. Please, Jenna, will you forgive me? I was in a bad place and I let that seriously affect my decision making skills."

"Of course, Carter, and the same goes for me. Now what in the heck happened here?"

Carter relayed the happenings of how everything had gone down. Together, the two attorneys came up with a plan on how to fix it. Jenna was able to pull a few strings with a friend at the district attorney's office, and within an hour, Jenna was the master he knew she was and it was looking as if this little event would not even show up on his record.

"It is a good thing you decided not to take that breathalyzer," Jenna said. "Good call. I may have had a harder time pulling the strings if you had."

"What?" Carter asked in confusion. "I did blow the test."

"Well, it didn't get logged then. Someone is looking out for you." As Carter gathered his belongings at the window, Jenna waited near the exit. Jamison Cross spotted Carter at the window and walked over to the older man.

"Well, the fact that you are walking out of this place today says to me that God may be looking out for you after all. I would venture to say He even cares about you, Carter Haggerty." Carter smiled at Jamison Cross, reached over, and gave the man a big hug. Carter, who was thin but not a small man, was dwarfed in the hug of the officer. From the corner, Jenna thought this was even more peculiar than the friendly conversation from before.

"Well, this better mean I am gonna see you at church next week. Or, there is always Monday night men's Bible study," Jamison said. "I think you have some thanks to give to God about this. I don't know that I have ever seen strings pulled that rapidly before."

"I will think about it," Carter said. Jamison smiled and gave him the address. With that, Carter Haggerty left the PPD in hopes to never return on the wrong side of the law.

"Hey, one more thing Carter," said Jenna. "I am gonna need you to stay near the area for a couple of days. I will work on tying up the loose ends, and by Friday afternoon, it should all be wiped away. It won't look good if you leave town, however, so stick around. She had no knowledge of what Carter was going to be missing if he stayed in Portland. However, Carter was starting to think there was something going on here. And he was wondering if Trinity Full Gospel was where he would find his answers.

Chapter 32

Church was a little hectic that morning. John had to work at 11:00. Blake was on the worship team and Tracy Cobalt, who was supposed to be Anna's helper, texted her early. Jenny Cobalt was having trouble with her asthma again. Tracy said she didn't dare take her out into the cold, or she had a feeling it would land her in the hospital again. The new medication had been working a lot better, but this cold weather was a killer. Ben was Anna's saving grace, gathering a couple of his friends and entertaining the kids before and after her message. Delaney came into the service for the first half hour and helped her lead worship. Collin went to the service with his mom, and even his sister decided to come to church. Delaney had heard that it was because Jax, Collin's best friend, was there—ah, young love.

New Year's Eve tomorrow would be filled with the rehearsal lunch that they had opted for instead of a dinner, followed by a church game night to ring in the New Year's holiday. Anna was thankful she had been able to get a break and rest up at the beach before the craziness. Lunch today would be McDonald's for sure, and then a nap. Anna scoured the church for her kids. Ben was easy to find; he was in the church's kids' room shooting mini hoops with his best friend Lucas. Blake she finally found in the sanctuary jamming on stage with a group of his kids. They were playing old rock ballads from the '80s, and since the church was at this point virtually empty except for the culprits on the stage, they had not been told to stop.

Anna loved that this group of kids all had each other. They weren't out drinking, doing drugs, and sleeping around, so Anna figure if a little old rock and roll in the sanctuary was the worst they were doing, she wasn't going to kill the mood. It was her day to lock up the building, but one of the older teens had worked as the church janitor for a while and knew the alarm code, so she wasn't even going to kick them out.

"Okay Blake, we're headed out. Are you ready?"

"I brought my own car, Mom. I will just meet you at home."

Anna might never get used to those words, *I drove here*. She had completely forgotten that he had come early for worship practice.

"Okay," Anna said. "All the doors are locked. Jeffrey, can you just set the alarm when you're finished? Blake and Carson, will you two please make sure all the sound equipment is off? And

Teresa, you keep these boys in line, and get the lights. I am out of here! Prayer meets at 6:00 so don't make a mess. But if any of you are hungry, head to McDonald's and I will get you a burger." She could hear the instruments shuffling around and the power being cut in the sanctuary as she walked out. Nothing could motivate teenagers faster than free food.

Collin, Delaney, Riley, Dolores, Franklin, Lacey, Cara, and Jax all headed to the little Mexican restaurant for lunch after church. Collin was still having a hard time believing this was all real. Riley was sitting on his lap dipping his fingers into the refried beans. Delaney reached over to the small child and wiped his fingers, handing him a curvy looking cookie thing.

"Here you go, buddy," she said. "Let's not make a mess, okay? You will get Daddy all dirty." Collin looked up at Delaney when she said those words and his heart swelled with love for her and love for this child. Delaney was such an amazing mother. Collin was not going to miss any more of his son's life. He and Delaney were going to do this together from now on.

Everyone had their food and was eating. Cara settled for a plate of salad and some corn tortilla shells.

"When did you decide to go vegan?" Delaney asked her curiously.

"After you left," was all Cara said. But Delaney could feel the tension at the table all of the sudden. Her leaving, she was starting to realize, had really done a number on many people, but Cara had really taken it hard. Delaney noticed how thin Cara was looking, a little bit on the unhealthy side of the fence. Delaney made a mental note to ask her about it more in depth after the wedding. The discomfort of the question dissipated quickly as Cara jumped right back into her shameless flirting with Jax. Poor Jax may not have a chance against that girl.

As the meal wrapped up, Franklin managed to swipe the check and foot the bill. He looked around the room. He could not be any happier than he was right at this moment. His wife looked even more beautiful to him than she had yesterday; the light had returned to her eyes. She was his Dory again, and he was so thankful. He looked at Collin and little Riley and, as much as he was a little afraid of the fact that the kids were so young, and that it would not be easy, Franklin knew it was all going to be okay. Something amazing was happening here and Franklin could not pinpoint what it was. Whatever it was, however, Franklin was excited to see what would come next.

Monday morning, Carter woke up feeling heavy. He knew he had a crazy road ahead of him. Yet, he couldn't help but remember what Officer Cross had said: *Remember, Trinity Full Gospel, somewhere on 19th Street downtown.* Well, if Carter couldn't go to Washington to fix the damage he had created with his son, he may as well head to the men's Bible study tonight and begin some work on himself. Carter Googled the times for the study and rechecked the address. Now, what was he going to do with himself until then? Carter walked back over to his computer, logged into his and his son's joint account which was now down to $394.72, and put back the money he had removed. Carter did not want to be lonely. He did not want to give up on his relationship with his son. Suddenly, Carter had a thought. He wanted to know his grandson. And for the second time in twenty-four hours, Carter began to pray, but this time in the privacy of his own home. Carter let the tears flow freely. Like the men in that prison cell who, on any given day would have been judged harshly by Carter Haggerty, Carter had judged his own son the day Collin decided to follow God and not his father. Carter was sorry. He now saw something different in Collin. And he wanted that for himself. If he was not mistaken, that something was God.

Chapter 33

Everything was coming together, and Delaney truly believed it was a God thing. The cake and the flowers would be added in when they arrived tomorrow morning, but besides that, everything looked magical. They had draped shimmery white cloth down the high wall from the cat walk in the sanctuary that shone cerulean blue in the projection of the lights. There was a beautiful arbor center stage, covered in tulle, glitter, and snowflakes, that was simply stunning. The perfectly place candelabra with the ice blue candles would be gorgeous when lit. The rehearsal was done. Everything had run like clockwork. Delaney sat on the front pew and stared hopefully at the set ahead of her. She felt, more than saw, Collin come up and sit in the pew behind her. She could smell his cologne and knew it was him.

"Are you sure you are ready for this?" He asked. "If you're going to change your mind, now is the chance."

Delaney angled her body in the seat so she could turn and see him. "I should be asking you that question," she said. "I am the girl with the baby whose life is different now, no matter what. You still have a choice, for about eighteen more hours.

Are you sure you are willing to give up on your dreams for me?"

"You are my dream," Collin said. "Also, the strangest thing happened today. I went to check my account to make sure I had enough money to cover ice skating tonight with Jax and Cara, and my account had been restored. Even my college money for next term was back. It is so strange, Delaney. It is not about the money, but to know that just maybe my dad is coming around to the idea of everything. That is amazing. I love you, Delaney Evans, and I want to spend the rest of my life telling you that. I have no idea what I am doing, but I want to be the best dad I can be to Riley, and I know that with God's help, we will be just fine. But knowing that my dad is considering not stepping out on me—that means a lot too."

Delaney's eyes were welling up, and so were Collin's. Collin reached over the pew in front of him and cupped the back of Delaney's head. Leaning in, he kissed her. The passion between these two was still incredible. Neither one of them could wait for tomorrow.

Everyone else had headed out to the Boathouse Restaurant for the rehearsal dinner. Lacey had decided that the Boathouse was the nicest restaurant in the area, and she had really wanted to keep it close to town. Dinner was lovely, and the service was fantastic. Collin and Delaney showed up just in time to place their orders of fish and chips. Jessica, Anna, and John were there with the kids, who would be singing at the wedding. Jax and Cara were also there. It was perfect. *How could we ask for more?* Delaney thought. And then she thought of Carter Haggerty. Delaney knew in her heart that he was not coming. The hope, however, was alive that one day Carter would come around. Delaney would be praying for that, as she knew Collin would be doing as well.

Carter stood in front of the doors of Trinity Full Gospel with no idea of what to expect. He really hoped Jamison Cross would be in attendance this evening. Carter was so confused about everything. He knew he needed change, and he was sure he had felt the pursuit of God, but what was he doing here in some inner city church? Carter had not wanted to just show up at some church near his town where he may run into someone he knew, that he was sure of; but it was more than that. There had been something so real about Jamison. Something he liked, something he wanted people to see in himself. He walked into the doors and was greeted by a man in his late sixties maybe.

"Hello sir, I am Hank. How can I help you?"

"I am here for your men's ministries meeting tonight."

"Ah yes. I am on my way there myself. Follow me, brother." Carter felt so strange. This was most definitely not his usual stomping grounds. Carter could not actually think of one black person that he had ever spent time with on a social level—or on any level really, ever. Yet, he felt like he was supposed to be here right now. Carter followed Hank into a room with about twelve other black men and two young white guys. Carter found a chair. Jamison was not here, but Carter refused to leave now, Jamison or no Jamison. Carter was going to find God tonight. And then, low and behold, through the doors Jamison walked in. He spotted Carter first thing and came and pulled up a chair beside him.

"Well, I'll be," Jamison said out loud. "I never thought you would actually show up, Carter, But I am so glad you are here." Jamison greeted several of the other men around the room. Then they all went around in a circle and introduced themselves to Carter.

Now it was Carter's turn.

"What brings you out here to us this fine evening, Mr. Carter?" With that invitation, Carter spilled it all—the story of Delaney running away, his son finding Jesus, them finding each other, and there being a ten month old baby in the picture. He added the fact that tomorrow was the wedding and that he could not leave town to attend because of his own stupid drinking and driving, after nearly cheating on his wife with a woman half his age.

Twenty minutes later, the men of the group had all listened intently to the story and were now laying hands on their white brother, praying for his situation. Hank closed the prayer. "Father God," he implored, "if there is any way you can open the door for my brother Carter to get himself to his son's wedding tomorrow, I pray you would open that door. Shove his behind through a window if you have to! Just get him there, God." And the men in the group all agreed, "Amen."

After they had prayed for Carter, Jamison was the one who asked the question that Carter had needed to be asked. "Have you given your life to Jesus, Carter?" Jamison inquired. "Have you decided to make the change to follow the Lord?" Carter shook his head no, and Jamison continued. "You know, there is a division between God and man. It is called *sin*. Sin creeps in and pushes us further and further away from the God that made and loves us. Jesus, He died on a cross to bridge that chasm. All you need to do is let the Lord know you screwed up and that you believe that He is God, and He is God enough to fix it all. When you confess with your mouth that Jesus is Lord, and believe in your heart that he died to save you, then you tell Him your sins and ask Him to take 'em away. He does it. As far as the east is from the west!" There was a chorus of *amen*'s and *you know that's right*'s, all around the room. Carter was suddenly certain that he was in the right place and that God Himself had brought him there. And in that moment, with a group of men he did not know, Carter committed his life to a God whom two days ago he had resented.

The rest of the meeting was filled with stories of God's provision and trust in God for the situations that seemed bleak. One man spoke of his and his wife's marital problems and how they had gone to a marriage encounter retreat and were making progress and falling in love all over again. Another man spoke about how his son, who had gotten into the gang scene and was doing some drugs, had agreed to go into rehab and was trying to turn his life to Jesus because he had hit rock bottom. Jamison shared of his daughter Keisha, who had heart surgery just weeks ago, and had not been doing so great. She was in and out of Doernbecher

Children's Hospital and the bills were really adding up. Carter's heart broke for the guy and once again, as for each situation, the group of men prayed. What had his wife said about his grandson? Heart problems, just like this little Keisha?

After praying, the men studied a passage in Matthew about God not crushing a man when he was down. Some of the scripture reading went over Carter's head, but he felt a yearning in his heart at the part where it went something like, *a bruised reed he would not crush and a smoldering wick he would not snuff out.* The men prayed one last time and committed to keep each other in prayer throughout the week.

Lacey had decided to head to the hot tub to let some of the stress melt away. She took her phone with her just in case Carter tried to call her. Lacey put her towel on a lounge chair and sat her phone down on top of it. She slowly stepped into the water and sat down. The water felt so good. Between the stress of the wedding and finding out about Delaney and the baby, and the stress of not knowing if her husband was ever going to come around, Lacey was one bundle of nerves. Carter had been so distant and cold lately. Lacey always thought she could handle it—she was a big girl. But

Cara needed her dad to be there for her. She could feel that they were losing her. And honestly, it was different than losing Collin. Collin had not been lost, but redirected. Cara *felt* lost.

Lacey was lost in her thoughts and didn't notice Dolores until she was stepping foot into the tub.

"Hello, friend," Dolores said.

"Hey there."

Dolores worked her way into the water and sat across from Lacey. "It has been a crazy week, hasn't it?" Dolores asked.

"Sure has," Lacey agreed. "Dolores, I wanted to say I am sorry. We have been friends for a long time. When Delaney left, I felt like I was not there for you like a friend should be. These last couple of days, I have realized how much I miss our friendship. I am thankful for you. I am really glad we are going to be in-laws together."

Dolores, looking at Lacey, said, "Well, it was not just you. I didn't handle the disappearance very well. I withdrew from everyone and everything. I am thankful to have you back, my friend."

"It is exciting to see how things are going with the kids. I am rather mesmerized by their new found faith," Lacey said. "It reminds me of the days I used to go to church with my family before Carter and I were married. I am not sure what happened to me. But I am so glad that God brought them to find faith before they found each other again."

"You know," Dolores said, "I am a little confused about this whole God thing. Don't get me wrong—we have always gone to church over the years, but this thing with Delaney and Collin seems so much more real. Even watching their new friends Anna and Jessica, it seems like there is something more that I am missing."

"I totally hear you and feel the same way," Lacey agreed. "I abandoned my faith a long time ago. I believe it is time for some reconnection between me and God. Carter may have an issue with it, but we have done things his way for a lot of years now. Quite frankly, it is just not working out for me. I think it is time for me to try doing things God's way again."

Dolores and Lacey spent the next twenty minutes in the hot tub discussing life and deciding that together, they were going to explore this God thing. The ladies rose out of the hot tub and reached for their towels. Lacey grabbed for her phone, and heard the dreadful thud and a splash as her cell phone went into the tub.

"Oh, man!" Dolores stepped into the water and retrieved the phone, quickly popping off its back and pulling out the battery. "You are going to need a bag of rice," she continued.

With that, the two ladies and the sopping phone headed on a mission to find that rice.

When Carter arrived home, he felt like the right thing to do would be to call his wife. Somehow, he had to be the bigger man and face the consequences to his horrible choices. Carter breathed a prayerful plea for help from the Lord as he picked up the phone. He really had so much to apologize for. He needed forgiveness for years and years of tearing down his wife and her beliefs. He wondered at this point why in the world Lacey had stuck with him. He had become a self-centered, self-absorbed jerk. It was crazy, the revelations he was witnessing that showed him the kind of person he had become. He did not deserve Lacey's devotion to him. And he was dreading the heart break that he was about to bring his wife. Until now, the one thing he had been was faithful.

Oh God, help me. Carter touched Lacey's name in his contact list. Her phone went straight to voicemail. Carter hung up and walked over to the water tap and ran a cold glass of water. He drank down the water and then dialed the phone again. He heard her voicemail greeting again, recorded in Cara's voice. *"Hey, this is Lacey Haggerty's phone, and she is unavailable. Leave her a message and I will help her retrieve it when I get home."* There was a little chuckle from his daughter, and then the beep signifying it was his time to talk. Just last week, Cara had recorded that message on her mom's voicemail. Carter had just told his wife on Christmas Eve when he had called to say he was running late from work, that the message was inappropriate for a woman of her class and age. Defeated and sad, Lacey had said she would take care of it. Right now, Carter was glad she hadn't. Hearing Cara's voice on the line had sure been easier than hearing the voice of his wife. At the beep, Carter left a message.

"Lacey, I have run into a bit of trouble and I am fairly sure that without a miracle, I will not be making it to our son's wedding. Please tell him I am sorry. And I will make it up to him somehow, if that is even possible. I am sorry Lacey, I am sorry I have sucked as a husband and as a father for the last twenty-plus years. I hope when you get home we can spend some time talking. I have so much to tell you. I love you, Lacey. And again, I am sorry."

Here it was, the morning of the wedding. Anna was hanging the last of the window coverings on the doors in the bride's changing room. It was 9:00 a.m., and in about an hour the wedding party would start to show up. *Life is funny sometimes,* Anna thought, *how God uses crazy things to turn people's lives around.* What an amazing grace she saw in the story of Delaney and Collin. Anna thought about the stories and the chapters in her own life, how God had taken turbulent waters and stormy seas and used them to bring about change, compassion, character, and often hope in her life. Whether peace like a river flowed or sorrows like sea billows rolled, Anna had truly learned that it was well with her soul. God was good always, and he was going to look out for these two young people. Anna could just feel it. God had an amazing plan for these kids, and it was going to revolve around their story. And until the day it came to pass, Anna could see them learning that they could have peace in turbulence. *It is well with my soul*—an often difficult but always beneficial lesson to learn.

Carter woke up to the phone ringing on his night stand Tuesday morning. Carter was amazed that he had been startled awake. He had not slept so deeply for years. He had gone to bed praying that somehow God would intervene in his situation. Collin looked at the caller ID and saw it was Jenna. With a bit of dread and a lot of anticipation, Carter answered the phone.

"Hello?" He said.

"Good morning, Carter. I just wanted to let you know that as of 30 minutes ago, your problem has been resolved. It is all water under the bridge. It looks as though it will not even end up as a stain on your record. I do not know how the district attorney managed to sequester the whole incident, but it has been done. You are free and clear."

Carter had a pretty good idea how it had all been eliminated; he had a pretty strong feeling that his new friend Jesus had something to do with it.

"Thanks so much, Jenna, praise the Lord. I am so thankful. I owe you one." Carter finished the rest of the short conversation with Jenna Jones and jumped into the shower. It was 9:15 and if he made it snappy, he just might make it to the church on time.

Collin woke up, jumped into the shower, and practically ran out the door of his hotel room. Delaney had taken all of the things he would need to get ready for the big day and had deposited them in the men's dressing room at the church. His excitement was palpable. Yet the thought that his dad would not be there today tainted the sweetness with a bitter aftertaste. *I will not let his choices ruin my day,* he thought, followed by a prayer that even if it was not today, that someday his father would come around. Collin felt a pang of hope as he thought about the mysterious return of his school money. Maybe there was hope, after all.

As he passed the Bremerton air strip, Collin thought about how, in just a few short hours, he and Delaney would be on a plane headed to Cali. The trip to Disneyland had been Cara's idea, and he could not wait to surprise Delaney with a trip to the happiest place on earth. Riley would be staying with Jessica and Anna, alternating days and nights. Having Jessica in the picture was the only way Delaney had agreed not to drag their son to their honeymoon with them. But honestly, Collin really wanted to have Delaney all to himself for the next week.

Bless his mother's heart—she had completely funded the trip from her savings account so that Collin's dad would not be upset. Delaney had also told him she was willing to pitch in with her newly inherited college fund her parents had given to her. College was looking a ways off for Delaney, and she said she would pay herself back. But then, Collin had somehow gotten all his money back. So there were now no money worries for him to stress about. How had this all worked out? Was it really a little less than a month ago that Collin had spotted Delaney from the O'Reilly's parking lot? Collin had been up until 2:00 this morning finishing writing his vows for today. He was a little nervous, but God was good and nothing was going to dampen his happiness today. Collin was almost there. His future lay just beyond this stop light. He couldn't wait!

Carter made a few phone calls as he threw on a suit and packed a few things into a small duffle he had found in his daughter's closet. Then he headed to PDX. Carter had procured the use of a small plane owned by his company, and had called ahead to have a taxi waiting to take him to the air strip. Finally, by 12:20 p.m., Carter was in the air and on his way to Bremerton. He was going to make it; he just knew it.

Delaney was in her room dressed and ready to go at 1:15 when she heard a tap on the door. Her mother, Anna, and Jessica were all in the room and had been helping her. Cara was busy primping to make herself beautiful for Jax. Dolores opened the door to find Delaney's father on the other side. He was escorted into the room and all of the ladies, even Cara, went out into the lobby of the church.

Franklin Haggerty walked over to his only daughter. "You look stunning, Delaney. I just wanted to say, I am so proud of you. I understand how hard this year was for you and I know that even though I wish it had all happened in a different way, I understand why you did it. I love you so much, and I am so thankful you are back in my life. I was a little lost without you, I must admit."

Delaney reached out to her father and he took her in his arms. "Thanks, Daddy!"

Franklin continued. "I want you to know that no matter what you and Collin decide to do in the future, I will be here to support your efforts. You know I am you biggest fan."

"I love you, Daddy, and you know what I think? I do have a new dream. I think I want to find a way to help people like me who are lost in these situations, young and scared. I want to help them and I want to show them the way to Jesus."

Franklin Evans had tears in his eyes now. He didn't know if he had fully bought into this Jesus thing, but he was bought in hook, line, and sinker to helping his daughter fix the problems of the world.

"I can do school locally and online, and still be a good mom. I want to be a counselor, Dad. I want to help people."

Franklin's heart swelled; he had raised one amazing daughter.

Jax walked up to Collin and put his arm around his shoulder. "Man," he said, "I am sorry your dad didn't make it. I prayed all night that he would."

"It's okay, man. I got my Christmas miracle. I will have to settle for that, but promise me you won't stop praying for my dad. He is so lost; you know he needs Jesus."

"I promise I won't stop. Well, it is time. Are you ready?"

"Ready as I will ever be."

Collin turned around to walk out the door and was instantly stunned. There in the doorway with his eyes full of tears stood his father. Jax backed into the corner as Carter Haggerty, the man who was as big as life, walked in the door.

"Collin, I am so sorry. I know, son, that you have been praying for me and yesterday, at Trinity Full Gospel Church, I gave my heart to Jesus."

Collin ran to his father and threw his arms around him "Oh, Dad. I love you. Thanks for making it."

"Well, let's do this thing. It is time for you to get in that sanctuary and marry that girl. I still think you are crazy, but I know you are also smart so you will make it work."

"Hey Dad, one last thing. Are you still willing to pay for law school even if I am married?"

"Are you kidding me here?"

"No, but I don't want to work for the firm, Dad. I think I have a brilliant plan of my own."

"Any plan that makes you a future attorney definitely has my attention, son. But this conversation might be better had after your honeymoon. Just know, I realize I have a lot to make up for in the dad department. And whatever plans you have, I will support you one hundred percent."

Collin gave his dad a big hug, and with that the two men walked to the sanctuary with Jax following closely behind. Then, Carter Haggerty took his place next to his daughter and his obviously shocked wife.

"Well that went well," Jax said. "God has been listening to your prayers. I have to admit, I was afraid nothing could penetrate the wall around the great Carter Haggerty."

Chapter 34

The moment was here. Delaney stood in front of the full-length mirror Anna had placed for her in the small room where she and the other ladies had gotten ready. Her floor-length white gown was stunning with its shimmering, ice blue, semi-translucent ice crystals sewn in. Her long blonde hair cascaded down her back in loose, perfectly shaped ringlets. Her makeup was perfect, with hints of shimmer here and there. Her look was classic, and not the least bit gaudy. Delaney had always been into simplicity when it came to her cosmetics and her accessories. Around her neck, she wore a beautiful snowflake necklace that Collin had gotten for her at Macy's earlier this week. Around her ankle, she wore an old beaded necklace that had belonged to her grandmother. The ice blue beads had gone with the wedding theme, and it was one of the few jewelry items Delaney had taken with her when she left home. The beads signified something old and something blue, as far as she was concerned. Around her wrist Delaney fingered a single Pandora bead on a chain. Her mother had let her borrow it, because the rose gold primrose signified new life for her and Collin and well as for her own parents. Her mother had explained the situation to her as she had fastened it to Delaney's wrist. The bracelet was both borrowed and new.

Something old, something new, something borrowed, something blue. Boom, all covered.

Franklin came up beside Delaney and grabbed her hand. The James boys, Ben and Blake, had already seated the mothers.

"Are you ready for this, my little moonbeam?" He asked as they stood staring at the door. The music was now at the part where the groom was supposed to enter. Pachelbel's Canon was playing beautifully; Delaney could picture Cara beaming as she walked in with Jax, followed by Jessica who was escorted by John James.

Her father opened the door when the time was right, and Delaney guided her full skirt through the doorway. Delaney watched as Brooklyn James, in her beautiful ice blue chiffon dress, dropped blue and white primrose pedals on the floor along the white runner, herding her little cousin Carson up the runway. He was adorable in his little tux as he happily tossed his ring bearer pillow up in air.

Suddenly, the music changed. Delaney and her father began to walk through the doorway into the sanctuary as all in attendance rose to their feet. Delaney could remember singing this song out under the golden chain tree in her childhood backyard. Each June the tree bloomed. One time

Delaney imagined it was her wedding day as she pretended to march down the aisle singing *here comes the bride, all dressed in white.* She then imagined dancing around under the green leaves and dropping golden yellow flowers. It was hard to believe that today was her and Collins day. She was a lucky girl.

As she walked down the rows, she passed a few high school friends she had not seen in years—friends she hadn't even realized were invited. She looked at her dad, who looked knowingly back at her.

"Your mother wanted to surprise you," he told her. "She wanted you to have friends at your wedding." Delaney spotted her best friend Natalie in the audience, and tears began to fall.

"My mom rocks," she told her dad.

"Yes, she really does," her father agreed. When Delaney and her father neared the front of the church, she was dumbstruck when she spotted Carter Haggerty sitting with his wife, who honestly looked equally dumbfounded. Carter made eye contact with her, and she felt warmth emanating from him that she had certainly never felt before. Then he smiled at her and Delaney knew that God had answered Collins prayers.

When the two of them reached the front of the stage, Delaney heard Anna's voice say, "Who gives this woman away to be married today?"

Her father spoke up. "Her mother and I do." Then, just like that, Franklin took his daughter's hand and placed it into Collin's.

"Friends and family, we are gathered here today to celebrate the joining together of two hearts," Anna began. "This captivating love story is different from many love stories we may know. This love story tells of two hearts separated by circumstances. Two hearts that through storms, troubles, and trials, never lost each other. This is a love that never faded through distance and misconstrued circumstances. This love between Collin and Delaney is indeed a 1 Corinthians 13 kind of love. It is a love that is patient, a love that is kind. A love that does not envy or boast. Their love is not proud. It does not dishonor others, and definitely is not self-seeking. This love is not easily angered, and keeps no record of wrongs. This love does not delight in evil, but rejoices with the truth. It most definitely seems to always protect, always trust, always hope, and I believe this love will always persevere. Because of this, love from God never fails.

"Delaney and Collin, I have grown to love the both of you. I know you are going to do great things for the Lord. With God's help, you will love and cherish each other. The vow you are making today will not always be easy to keep. But as you stand here today, you are agreeing that you will work together to make this lifelong bond work!

Collin looked into the eyes of this beautiful woman he loved so much. His heart was full. "I love you, Delaney, and I always will."

"I love you too, Collin Haggerty," Delaney whispered back.

Anna continued. "Delaney and Collin have chosen to write their own vows to each other, so at this time, we are going to let them speak those vows."

Delaney handed her flowers to Jessica and took the microphone from Anna

"Collin Haggerty, if I have discovered anything about life in the last year, and I have, I now know for a fact, that I do not want to live another season of life without you.

"No matter what you decide to do with your life, whether God calls you to be a preacher, a lawyer, or a cab driver, I will follow you and support you with all I am. I will love you, take care of you, make you soup when you're sick, and rub your shoulders when you are weary. I will laugh at your jokes and cry when you are hurting.

"I will stand beside you, for richer and for poorer. I will trust you with my heart, because you are the most kind and gentle man I have ever known. I love you, Collin, and I can't wait to spend the rest of my life showing you just how much."

Delaney smiled at Collin, whose eyes were full of unshed tears. "I love you," she said, and then she handed him the mic.

"Delaney Evans, it is hard to comprehend just how much I love you. You are my best friend. Our love is so strong. I truly believe we can accomplish anything if we do it together.

"Today I pledge myself to you in marriage. You have taught me what it is to love someone so deeply that you never give up on the hope that you have to be with her forever.

"I commit to you today to love you with all of my heart. I promise to protect your life with mine and to be the best husband and father I can be.

"I want to celebrate with you in all of the good times, and I want to stand next to you in the tough times. And during life's deepest sorrows, I will be there to carry you as together we trust in Jesus to get through those sorrows together. In health, I will thrive with you, and when sickness crosses our path, I will be right by your side. I promise this from now until the day that I breathe my last breath.

"Rich or poor, who cares? We will figure it out. We have the Lord and He will take care of us. Delaney, from the day we started to hang out, when we were so young, I knew that you were special. You are the only one for me, and I never ever want to be apart from you again. I love you, and I can't wait to spend the rest of my life loving you."

Anna took the mic back from Collin. "Now the couple would like you to pray with them as they take their first communion together as a married couple and as they join the fires of the unity candle."

The music began to play as Blake and Ben James sang a beautiful rendition of "It Is Well". There was not a dry eye in the house as the couple walked over and joined their two candles to light the giant ice blue candle under the snow flake arbor center stage.

As the song finished, Delaney and Collin rose from the kneeling position they were in and again took their places in front of Anna.

Anna turned to Delaney first. "Do you, Delaney Evans, take Collin Haggerty to be your husband?"

"I do," Delaney replied with a soft sweetness that still held conviction.

"Do you, Collin Haggerty, take Delaney Evans to be your wife?"

"I do."

"Then, by the power vested in me by God and the state of Washington, I now pronounce you man and wife. Collin, you may kiss your bride."

There was a roar of applause and cries of *woohoo* from Collin's college friends as Collin leaned down and drew Delaney into the most beautifully passionate yet tasteful kiss.

Anna beamed. "I would like to present to you Mr. and Mrs. Haggerty!" The song "I'm a Believer" began to play and Collin scooped a screaming, giggling Delaney up into his arms and half-jogged her down the aisle, putting her down at the back of the door to greet the guests that Anna dismissed methodically.

The receiving line went slowly, despite the fact that there were only about 80 people in attendance. As the line dissipated, Delaney took her father's hand and Collin, his mother's, and they walked down the stairs to the fellowship hall.

Delaney had always dreamed of the dance she would share with her daddy on her wedding day. As the music began, her father led her to the small wooded dance floor that had been laid in the hall the night before. Peering from the corner of her eye, she saw Collin also preparing to share a similar moment with his mother. The DJ announced the start of the dance that the couples would share with their father and mother. Franklin looked into Delaney's eyes and felt disbelief that a week ago, they had still been separated. Something was happening here. Franklin had a feeling many great things were to come. Looking into the eyes of his only daughter, a tear formed in his eye. He pulled Delaney close to himself and he heard her sigh in his ear. The smell of the Love Spell perfume she had always loved filled his senses and he was transported back to those years when everything seemed so simple. He was suddenly dancing the dances they had shared at daddy-daughter events in the past. His baby had grown up to be such a beautiful young lady!

He was awoken from his memories by his daughter's soft, sweet voice tickling his ear. "I love you, Daddy," Delaney whispered. "I am so sorry. Thank you for never giving up on me! Thank you for your help, even when you could have given up hope."

"I would never have given up on you. With the orange of every sunrise and the red of each sunset, my hope in finding you grew. I am pretty sure it may have been the Lord renewing that hope. I am believing for great things from you, little moonbeam. I think just maybe God has a special plan for your new little family."

"I love you, Daddy. I am one blessed girl."

Lacey and Collin danced over and Lacey handed her son over to Delaney. As Delaney settled into his longing arms, Lacey smiled.

"They're going to be just fine," Lacey told Franklin before they moved off the floor to join their spouses.

Franklin smiled at his long-time family friend. "I believe you are right."

The reception progressed. Cara about knocked out a couple other young ladies as she caught Delaney's bouquet of blue and white primroses. Then, in an attempt to duck out of the way, Jax managed to bend directly into the garter belt, catching it safely in his midsection. He did not even realize what he did until a couple of the guys began to chant his name.

The cake turned out simply beautiful, even prettier than the picture with the ice blue accents that had been added. The whole day was beautiful.

"I kind of don't want to leave for the honeymoon," Delaney whispered to her new husband as they made their way to the door. "I just got all of these people back, and I want to spend time with them all."

"Oh no, Mrs. Haggerty, you are all mine for five days."

"I am going to miss Riley so much."

"I know. So will I, but it is only five days, Mrs. Haggerty."

Delaney turned to Collin and gently kissed his lips. "Okay, Mr. Haggerty. But you may have to cheer me up a few times over the next five whole days."

"Oh honey, you are gonna be so happy you won't need any cheering. Not to mention you will be exhausted." Delaney playfully smacked his arm. "That is not even what I meant!" Collin laughed, "But, well, there is that too." He smiled.

Delaney took a moment to hug Natalie with a huge thanks for coming and a promise to call her as soon as she got back. Then she hugged Mrs. Haggerty and greeted Mr. Haggerty, who was teary and cheerful—weird. There was a hug for Cara and Anna and Jessica, accompanied with a "take good care of my baby," and them a tearful hug and kiss for her mom and dad. Collin also made his way through the last round of hugs and came to his parents.

"Mom, thanks for everything. I don't know what I would have done without you this week, and Dad, you don't know what it means to me that you showed up. I love you and, well, that would have broken my heart. Thanks Dad!"

"I love you son, and when you get back what do you say we get together and plan what we're going to do about your future?"

"Deal," Collin said, and he turned towards his bride. Hand in hand, they walked through the snowy walkway to the waiting limo while everyone they loved blew bubbles at them.

"Well, Mrs. Haggerty, here's to many years of adventures." Collin reached into the little bag he was carrying and pulled out a pair of Minnie Mouse ears. They read, *Mrs. Haggerty*. He placed them on Delaney's head and pulled out a matching *Mr. Haggerty* pair for himself.

"Well, what do you think? Are you ready to go to the happiest place on earth?" Collin asked Delaney.

"As long as I am with you, Collin Haggerty," she answered, "I will always be in the happiest place."

Made in the USA
Coppell, TX
19 November 2020